As she wonde... return, the doorknob rattled.

Melissa jolted upright and pulled her gun from its holster.

The door creaked open and Nick stepped inside. A sob of relief balled in her chest.

He wrapped his arms around her and pulled her to his chest. "It's okay. It's all okay."

She knew what he was saying must be true. He obviously hadn't been shot dead outside the corral. He was fine. But her brain somehow couldn't absorb the realization.

She tilted her head back and stretched her arms around his neck. It was idiotic. Stupid to feel this way, but she didn't care. She had to feel he was alive, that he was really there.

As they got closer, something opened inside her. Something strong and invincible...and more vulnerable than any feeling she'd ever known.

ANN VOSS PETERSON

A RANCHER'S BRAND OF JUSTICE

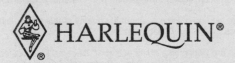

HARLEQUIN®

TORONTO • NEW YORK • LONDON
AMSTERDAM • PARIS • SYDNEY • HAMBURG
STOCKHOLM • ATHENS • TOKYO • MILAN • MADRID
PRAGUE • WARSAW • BUDAPEST • AUCKLAND

To Cole and Brett

Recycling programs
for this product may
not exist in your area.

ISBN-13: 978-0-373-69487-7

A RANCHER'S BRAND OF JUSTICE

Copyright © 2010 by Ann Voss Peterson

ABOUT THE AUTHOR

Ever since she was a little girl making her own books out of construction paper, Ann Voss Peterson wanted to write. So when it came time to choose a major at the University of Wisconsin, creative writing was her only choice. Of course, writing wasn't a *practical* choice—one needs to earn a living. So Ann found jobs, including proofreading legal transcripts, working with quarter horses and washing windows. But no matter how she earned her paycheck, she continued to write the type of stories that captured her heart and imagination—romantic suspense. Ann lives near Madison, Wisconsin, with her husband, her two young sons, her border collie and her quarter horse mare. Ann loves to hear from readers. E-mail her at ann@annvosspeterson.com or visit her Web site at www.annvosspeterson.com.

Books by Ann Voss Peterson

*Wedding Mission

CAST OF CHARACTERS

Nick Raymond—To this rancher, justice is all about getting his son back and being left alone.

Melissa Anderson—Devastated over the loss of a police detective friend, Melissa is personally dedicated to finding a murderer.

Jason Raymond—The innocent little boy is too young to be a credible witness. So why does someone want to hurt him?

Gayle Rodgers—Nick's ex-wife stole his son and disappeared three years ago. Now she has turned up dead.

Jimmy Bernard—Was the fallen detective a hero or a villain?

Tammy Bernard—Is the detective's wife too good to be true?

Jose Sanchez—Could the accused killer be trying to cover his tracks?

Essie Castillo—Is the victim's advocate the key to this whole case?

Seth Wallace—The deputy district attorney is sure to make certain he comes out of this mess smelling like a rose...one way or another.

Cory Calhoun—Is he a thorough investigator or a man seeking revenge?

Ben Marris—Does the detective want justice? Or does he have his own dirty secrets to hide?

Chapter One

Three long years he'd looked. Three years.

Staring at the parking garage's concrete wall, Nick Raymond gripped the steering wheel of his pickup to still his shaking hands. He'd spent half a fortune on a private investigator, mortgaging the ranch to pay his bill, and had come up with nothing. Not a trace.

Until yesterday.

He switched off the ignition and glanced into the backseat of his king cab. The seat belt was hooked into the booster seat. The DVD player was loaded with Disney movies for the long trip home, and the gas tank was full. He'd stocked up on snacks and juice boxes and had even picked up a stuffed buffalo. He was as ready as he was ever going to be.

He yanked the keys from the ignition. They jangled in his fingers and dropped to the floor mat.

He was a mess.

Leaning his forehead on the steering wheel, he pulled in a deep breath and let it out slowly. He hadn't been this nervous since the trip home from the hospital after Jason was born. Heart pounding and palms sweating, he'd been sure something horrible would happen to the little tyke on the road back to the ranch. Gayle had laughed at him, though she was just as anxious.

Gayle. A dull ache centered in his gut. He'd imagined finding her for three years, mapped out every bitter word he'd throw at her, every curse he'd level for stealing his son. And now, he'd forgive it all if she were here.

If she were still alive.

He still couldn't absorb that she'd been bludgeoned to death by a man who'd tried to rob her late at night in her own apartment. He hadn't even thought of funeral arrangements. He couldn't think of them now. Now he only wanted to focus on reuniting with Jason. On bringing his four-year-old son home.

He retrieved his keys and dismounted from the truck. Hitting the lock button on the remote, he strode through the parking structure, the thud of his boot heels echoing off concrete, heading for the nearest red exit sign. This nervous quake that had a hold of him was ridiculous, but he couldn't stop it.

Jason probably didn't remember his dad or the Circle J. Had he ever ridden a horse? Did he like horses? After spending the past three years in the city, would he hate living on the ranch as much as his mother had?

Nick made his way down two flights of stairs. Of course, he was getting ahead of himself where Jason was concerned. There was a lot to think about before he'd get a chance to introduce his son to life in Wyoming. A lot to sort out with the Denver police. A lot to move beyond. But no matter how long it took to cut through the red tape, Nick wouldn't be going back to the ranch alone. He would be bringing his boy with him.

And nervous as he was, that fact brought a grin to his face and a warmth to his chest that he would make sure he never lost again.

Breaking out onto the street, he squinted against Denver's mile-high sunshine. Even the day seemed to be celebrating his fresh beginning. The air felt dry and a little crisp, a taste of fast-approaching fall. The sky was blue. The city pulsing with energy. It was going to be a good day. He could feel it.

It had to be.

He'd memorized the map he'd printed out from the hotel's Web site, but he pulled the paper from his back pocket just the same. It rattled in his hand as he looked over the familiar two-block distance he'd walked in his mind countless times on the drive down from Wyoming.

A truck roared past spewing black exhaust into the air. A dog yapped from an apartment window. A dark blue car full of young tattooed men blasting music from open windows pulled to the curb behind him. He could see all of it. Hear all of it. But he couldn't seem to focus on anything. His mind was tuned totally to the hotel rising on the corner ahead, its colorful flags flapping in the breeze.

This was it.

For a second, his legs felt weak. Maybe he should have waited, met his son at the police station, the way the detective who'd called had wanted. But that had seemed so official. So dry. In that setting, Jason might be afraid of this man he didn't remember. And Nick didn't want to start out that way.

But now he wasn't sure this idea was better.

He glanced around. So much noise. So much bustle. This would confuse the boy for sure. And after all Jason had been through in the past few days, he'd probably had enough confusion. Nick needed to find a way to make things easier.

He was still more than half a block away when the light shifted on the glass doors leading into the hotel lobby. A broad-shouldered man wearing a sports jacket pushed his way out. He glanced from side to side, the sun sparkling on his gray hair and the nearly white mustache tickling his upper lip. At first he looked like a regular businessman, then a wind gust blew back his jacket, revealing a holster on his hip.

Nick's pulse spiked. The detective. It had to be. And that probably meant...

The man reached behind his back and grabbed the door handle, holding it open. A woman with golden-blond hair brushing her shoulders stepped out behind him, a small brown-haired boy at her side. Another woman followed behind, also dressed professionally, but Nick was no longer looking at the people surrounding his son.

His son.

A hum rose in his ears and the whole universe seemed to scope in until it included no movement, no sound, no city smells, nothing but him and the boy he'd been looking for for so long.

His son.

Jason's eyes flared wide as he took in the city street. From this distance, they looked blue, like his mother's. But everything else—the slope of his nose, the cleft in his little chin, the way his ears stuck out from his shorn head—all of it looked so much like photos of Nick at age four, that for a second he couldn't quite breathe.

His son.

He dodged around the few people on the sidewalk until no one was between him and his boy but the three people with him. A roar rose from somewhere far away. Something dark glided past him on the street. Someone shouted. But all he could see was Jason. All he could think about was reaching him. Hearing his voice. Taking him in his arms. Holding him and never letting him go.

He was still thirty yards away when the shooting started.

Chapter Two

Melissa Anderson had been on the force for ten years before she got her job as investigator with the district attorney's office, but except for training at the range, she'd never fired her gun. Not on the streets. Not for any reason.

But she knew what it sounded like.

The first shot was a sharp pop, the noise diffused by other noises and distance. But by the time the second exploded close up, she was already reacting.

She grabbed the boy, his little arm thin under her fingers. She had to get him out of the line of fire. She had to make sure he was safe. The hotel's glass doors wouldn't protect him much, but to the right a concrete planter sprouted from the sidewalk, red blooms cascading from the top. She half ran, half dove, dragging Jason with her. Her knees hit the sidewalk, the force shuddering up her legs and into her hips. Her hand scraped raw against concrete, breaking her fall and the boy's. She pushed him behind her, between the planter and the hotel wall, and reached for her gun.

Pulling it free from its holster, she froze, heart stuttering in her chest. Jimmy lay on the sidewalk. Essie behind him. Everything was eerily quiet.

She focused on the street. She was sure she'd seen a dark car from the corner of her eye. Maybe blue. She swore it was there when the shooting started. Now it was gone.

She shook her head, as if that would help her remember, help her sense where the car was now. Her mind was numb. She couldn't think. She couldn't feel.

Training. She had to rely on her training. Take one step, then another.

She checked the boy. His blue eyes were as wide as a mountain sky but he wasn't hurt. She reached for her cell phone. Her hands trembled. Her voice too high, too frantic. She called in what she'd seen. The words *officer down* stuck in her throat.

It couldn't be. It couldn't be. Not Jimmy.

Only seconds had passed, but it seemed like minutes. Hours. No movement from Jimmy or Essie.

"Where is he? Oh, my God. Is he okay?" A man in cowboy boots, jeans and a button-down shirt barreled down the sidewalk toward her.

Instinctively, she raised her weapon. "Stop."

He halted, staring at her. His hands splayed at his sides, his eyes wild. He glanced around. At Jimmy. At Essie. "Jason? Where's Jason?"

His words clicked into place in her mind. The father. He was the father. He wasn't supposed to be here. But he was. She lowered her gun. "Your son is behind me."

He took ragged steps toward her. "Is he hurt?"

"No." She shifted to the side. At least with the father there, she could rely on him to care for the boy. She could focus on helping Jimmy and Essie. Be ready in case the shooter circled back before backup arrived.

Oh, God. Could this really be happening? Heat welled up in her chest and flushed over her skin. She wanted to scream. She wanted to sob.

She forced the feelings down. Later she could absorb this. Now she had to do her job. She shifted to the side and peered at the boy.

Impossibly huge eyes stared back. Tears streaked little cheeks. His chin trembled and teeth chattered as if he was horribly cold.

She wanted to hug him, to hold him, to let him know everything would be all right. The boy needed all those things. She'd have to trust the father would provide them. "Remember the man we talked about, Jason? Your daddy?"

His head moved in an almost imperceptible nod.

"He's going to take care of you now."

The boy's hands closed around her arm.

"It's okay. It's okay. He loves you more than anything. He'll take good care of you." She didn't know why she said it. She just hoped it was true. "I have to go help Detective Bernard and Essie. They're hurt. I need you to be brave now. Do you understand?"

Another small nod.

She looked back to the father. After her promises to the boy, he'd better be up to the task. He'd better not let her down. "Take my place. Right now."

As she stepped out from behind the planter, he slid into the spot she'd vacated. Without looking back, she raced to Jimmy B.

He was lying on his side, curled inward, his gun still

in hand. She smelled the blood before she saw it. The copper-sweet tang clogged the back of her throat and mixed with her tears.

Jimmy was wearing his bullet-proof vest. He hadn't been hit in the head. So where was the blood coming from? She brought her fingers to his throat, feeling for a pulse. Her hand came away sticky.

No. No. No.

The neck. Maybe the upper chest. Vulnerable tissue the vest didn't cover. Not good. He had to live. He had to. What would she ever do without him?

She clawed his blazer out of the way and ripped open his shirt. His vest was intact. Not damaged in the least. And right above the top edge, blood pulsed from a hole in his upper chest.

Pulsing blood meant his heart was still beating. He was still alive.

She ripped free the Velcro holding the vest in place and shoved it to the side. She shucked her blazer and wadded it up, pressing it to the wound. Looking up from her mentor and friend, she scanned the sidewalks for help.

Several people stood fifty feet away, either too afraid to approach or too selfish to get involved. "Can I get a hand here?"

No one moved.

Damn. What was wrong with these people? "I have two people hurt here. I need assistance."

"I'm here." A deep voice came from behind her.

She spun around without lessening the pressure on Jimmy's chest. The boy's father stood over her, the morning sun glaring behind him, his face in shadow.

"Where's Jason?"

"Here. What can I do?"

She didn't want the boy to see this nightmare. Not after all he'd already been through. But she couldn't just let Essie lie there bleeding. Jimmy was still alive. Essie might be, too. She needed help. "Hold this. Keep up the pressure." She grabbed his rough hand and pressed it to the blazer, already sticky with blood.

The man hunkered down over Jimmy. The boy huddled behind his father, his side pressed to the man's hip as if they were attached. He held his hands over his face.

The sight hit Melissa like a kick to the chest.

Function. She couldn't let herself feel. She had to function.

Melissa moved to Essie. A victim's rights advocate with the D.A.'s office, Essie wasn't wearing a shred of Kevlar. The stain of blood spread over her blouse and seeped through her suit jacket. Melissa pulled back the jacket and fumbled with the blouse's lower buttons until she had it partially undone. She peeled saturated cotton away from skin and located the bullet wound.

She had to stop Essie's bleeding. She had to—

"Here." A woman's voice this time.

She looked up to see a maid from the hotel leaning over her. In her arms, she cradled a stack of bleached-white towels.

"Thank God."

Somewhere a siren screamed. Help was on its way. She just prayed it would come fast enough. She just prayed it wasn't already too late.

NICK'S HEAD STILL SPUN. The whole thing—from hearing that first explosion of gunfire to now, sitting in a nearly vacant hospital waiting room with Jason to see who wanted to question him next—made him feel like he was trapped in a surreal nightmare.

It hadn't taken long for a flood of police and rescue workers to reach them, even though it had felt like hours. From then until now, he had been ushered from one place to another, answering the same questions over and over, caught in a storm of activity over which he had about as much control as Jason did.

None.

He watched the two men standing near the waiting room's doorway, murmuring in argumentative voices too low for him to decipher. He'd talked to the one in the blue blazer, Detective Marris, for hours. The interview had been one way only, the man asking every question Nick could possibly imagine, but had answered none of Nick's. He'd even brought in a police artist who'd attempted to sketch the young men Nick had spotted in the car—the men who had sprayed the sidewalk with bullets moments later. The whole time, Marris had been selectively deaf, hearing Nick's answers but ignoring even the simplest question Nick asked. Even now, watching Marris arguing with an orange-haired D.A.'s investigator by the name of Calhoun, Nick felt that same wave of blind frustration building inside.

He pulled his gaze from the men and focused on the television suspended in the corner. Cartoon sound effects jangled through the room. Jason sat on the hard couch next to him, pudgy fingers clutching the book they must have read twenty times by now.

The pediatrician they'd seen when they'd first arrived at the hospital had given him a clean bill of health. The child psychologist they had seen next had said it might be a while before he could process everything. Nick didn't know what to think. He wished he could make things easier on the boy, but he didn't know how. He didn't know how to deal with all that had happened himself. All he did know was that he needed to get his son somewhere far away from all this.

Somewhere safe.

The conference room door swung open and the blonde who'd sheltered Jason on the sidewalk slipped into the room. Nick had been impressed with how controlled she'd been in the midst of his panic. How she'd told him what to do, watching out for Jason the whole time. How she'd immediately tried to save the people who'd been gunned down. How she'd calmly reported everything to the police who'd finally arrived at the hotel.

She didn't look so strong and in control now. Her face looked like porcelain, pale and brittle. Her eyes were red-rimmed and puffy. And instead of in charge, she seemed nearly invisible. As if her will had drained away. She walked past the bristling men without giving them a glance and slipped into the chair beside the sofa. She focused on Jason and offered him a tentative smile. "How are you holding up, Buddy?"

"Melissa."

Jason's tremulous lisp sliced through Nick.

The boy reached small hands out for her. "Melissa." He lurched forward, trying to reach her.

She glanced at Nick. "Do you mind if I hold him?"

"Please do." Whatever helped his son feel grounded was fine with Nick. Obviously the boy knew Melissa better than he knew his own dad.

Melissa reached out her hands and gathered him onto her lap. She wrapped her arms around him and hugged. There was a desperation to the gesture, as if she needed anchoring as much as Jason.

Silence stretched between them like a chasm, silence he itched with the need to bridge. "I'm not sure what happened out there, but I don't think we officially met. I'm Nick Raymond."

"Melissa Anderson."

He waited a beat for her to go on, to maybe throw him a bone of information, but she didn't. Finally he cleared his throat. "Thank you."

She tilted her head to the side and narrowed her eyes, as if she had no idea what he was talking about.

"For taking care of Jason. For saving…" He eyed his son, unsure of how much he should say.

"Of course." Her lips seemed to tremble. Then she pressed them together and sank back into silence.

Conversation had never been Nick's strong suit, not that it had been too much of a problem. Usually people were eager to talk. Whether it be a guest at the ranch or an acquaintance in town, all he had to do was give them a little eye contact, and they were on a verbal roll. He had no clue how to draw out information tactfully. He usually just blurted things, another one of his coarse habits that had driven Gayle crazy. "The people that were shot, are they okay?"

She watched him as if she thought he should already know the answer.

Nick nodded in the direction of the detective and investigator. "No one has told me anything."

Melissa pursed her lips into a tight line. For a moment he thought she was going to just leave his question hanging. Finally she let out a sigh. "The victim's advocate, Essie, is in surgery. They don't know if she'll make it or not." Her voice sounded as dry as a police report, the objective aloofness undercut by the trembling of her lips.

"And the detective?"

Her focus shifted away from his face and latched on to the television. "Jimmy died."

"I'm sorry."

She bobbed her head. Her mouth formed the word *thanks,* but no sound came.

He wished he could do something, say something. But he knew there was nothing to say. Jason had a better chance of bringing some kind of comfort with a hug than he could with all the words in the English language.

He watched his son nestle in Melissa's arms. Time ticked by, only the cartoon voices marking the change. Eventually Jason's eyelids started drooping, and he folded into sleep.

"If you want you can put him down here on the couch."

"I'd rather hold him. If that's okay with you."

"Sure."

She narrowed her eyes on him, scrutinizing him for so long, it was all he could do not to look away. "Has anyone told you what to expect? Where you'll be going from here?"

"I hoped we'd be going home."

She hesitated, as if unwilling to give him bad news.

"What is it?"

"Your son might be in danger."

"Which is why I want him out of here."

"And it isn't just about your son. How much did you see of the car? The shooters?"

The same questions he'd fielded from more people than he could keep straight. "I've already answered these questions."

"For police. I'm an investigator with the district attorney's office."

Like Calhoun. "What's the difference?"

"Different boss. Different office. Please, indulge me."

He let out a heavy breath. Why not? He'd gone over the details so many times already, he nearly had it memorized. "The car was a midnight-blue sedan with Colorado plates. There were four kids inside, maybe in their late teens or early twenties. They had tattoos on—"

"Ms. Anderson?" a male voice cut through his spiel before he could even get to the part about the police artist.

Nick turned toward the doorway. Marris and Calhoun were gone, replaced by a man wearing a nice suit. Green eyes so intense they were almost shocking focused on Melissa. "Can I speak to you?"

Melissa glanced to Nick. "Sorry." She carefully handed Jason over to Nick and pushed herself out of her chair. "I'll be right back."

Jason snuggled warm against his chest, his thumb jammed in his mouth with purpose, refusing to wake up. Nick strained to hear their murmured conversation from the hallway. But except for a somewhat startled expression on Melissa's face, he couldn't pick up any of the exchange.

Finally Melissa stepped back into the room. The well-dressed man followed tentatively behind her, as if entering the room wasn't his idea but hers. He glanced at Jason and then at Nick. "Mr. Raymond? I'm Chief Deputy District Attorney Seth Wallace."

Nick nodded a greeting.

Wallace gave him a tepid, white-toothed smile. "I'm sorry your son has had to go through this. I hope we can make your stay here in Denver comfortable, in light of the circumstances."

"My stay in Denver won't be long. I'm leaving today."

The man's brows arched toward sandy hair. "I'm afraid that's not possible. Your son is a witness to a murder. Now, I'm afraid you are, too. I'm going to request that you stay in the city, at least until we can determine what happened here. I'll do my best to arrange for protection."

"Protection?" Heat rushed to his face. He'd been careful to hold his tongue around Jason all day, not wanting to frighten his son even more. But with the little guy asleep, he didn't have to hold back. And now was certainly not the time to let tact get in the way. "Looks to me like you've already tried to provide protection. And it almost got my son killed."

"I'm sorry for what happened today. And rest assured that we are launching a separate investigation. We'll get to the bottom of this. You have my word on that. And it won't happen again. We'll keep your son safe, we'll keep you safe, and we'll make sure justice is done."

"I'm all for justice, but not if it endangers Jason."

"We'll be sure it doesn't."

Nick blew a derisive breath through his nose. "You must think I'm some kind of Wyoming rube."

"I assure you, that is not true. This district attorney's office takes your concerns seriously. Melissa and I take your concerns seriously. And I promise you, we will get to the bottom of this."

"I'd like to help you out. I really would. But not at the risk of my son's safety." Nick glanced from investigator to deputy district attorney. "What happened this morning is your problem. Mine is keeping my son safe, and I don't trust anyone in Denver when it comes to that."

"I know you don't want to hear this, sir, but I'm afraid I can't let either one of you go anywhere." He focused on Melissa. "You'll take them?"

She nodded.

No, no, no. After a day of waiting, things were suddenly going too fast. "Wait a second. Take us where?"

He glanced at the men in the mouth of the room. "A hotel. Think of it as a safe house, of sorts."

"Of sorts?"

"It's for your own protection."

"Whoa, whoa, whoa. You can't make me go anywhere."

"Actually, I can. Either you go with Detective Anderson right now, or I get a material witness warrant to hold you. How do you feel about a jail cell?"

Nick frowned. He liked to think he could keep up with city types, but he had to admit that without a law degree, he was no match for this guy. His gaze landed on Melissa Anderson. She might not be on his side, but he was pretty sure she was on Jason's. "This warrant will put me and my son in jail? Is that true?"

"You'll go to jail." She met his gaze with dispassion, but behind the mask, he thought he saw a glimmer of... sympathy...something. "For him, we'll have to make arrangements through child services."

So he wouldn't even be with Jason? "You can't do that."

The deputy D.A. shook his head. "I just told you, Mr. Raymond, we can."

He kept his attention on Melissa. If he looked at Wallace right now, he'd probably spring out of his chair and choke the lawyer with his own power tie. "I mean you can't do that to a kid who just lost his mother. He needs some stability. He needs to go home."

Melissa nodded. "And he'll be able to. Eventually. Once we get the chance to sort through a few things."

So much for his ally. He blew out a heavy breath.

"So what's it going to be Mr. Raymond? Jail? Or go quietly with Ms. Anderson?"

Nick looked to Melissa Anderson. His impression from earlier flitted into his mind. She was grief stricken over the police detective who'd died, suffering from the same adrenaline rush aftereffects as he was, and she had a soft spot for Jason. All things he might be able to use to manipulate her and slip away. Not that he was wild about taking advantage of her, but if it came down to choosing between her and getting his son the hell out of this town, his choice was an easy one. "Shall we leave, Ms. Anderson?

MELISSA PUSHED HERSELF OUT of the waiting-room chair. Looked like she was in for babysitter duty again. She'd like to say she resented it, but that wouldn't be true. She loved being with Jason. He was such a sweet kid, and the tragedy he'd been through broke her heart. Keeping him safe couldn't be higher on her list of priorities. But being around his father?

That she could live without.

It wasn't that she disliked him. Actually, the opposite. Something about those broad shoulders, the cowboy swagger in his gait, the sincerity in his eyes, and she had to admit, the way those jeans hugged slim hips… the whole package made her feel weak.

And there was nothing she hated more than feeling weak.

Exactly why she didn't want to be around him or anyone else right this moment. After Jimmy's death and with Essie hanging on to life by a thread, she was feeling anything but strong. She needed to get home, draw the blinds, curl up in the fetal position and lose it.

Alone.

But if what Seth Wallace suspected was true, she

had little choice. Jason needed her. And she would do whatever she had to in order to keep the four-year-old safe. And his father.

Besides, it would only be temporary.

They had just reached the lobby floor when Nick stopped. "We'd better use the restroom before we leave."

"All right." Melissa stretched out her arms for the boy.

"I think he might need the visit, as well."

She eyed Jason. His cheek flattened against Nick's shoulder, his mouth open, a little drool glistening on his lips and forming a wet spot on his father's shirt. "He's totally out."

"I'll wake him if I need to."

She shook her head. "We aren't going that far. I'm sure he can wait."

"No, it's better this way."

She wanted to ask who it was better for, but decided to let it go. If she thought she felt a little out of it, Nick Raymond was in undoubtedly worse shape. At least she worked around tough situations every day. Gang violence. Domestic abuse. Homicide. Nick was a cowboy. He was used to horses and wide-open spaces, not the tragedy of a modern city. Maybe the thought of being away from the son he'd just found again was too much for him. She could understand that. "All right. I'll wait here."

He touched the brim of his hat and nodded.

A little shiver ran up her spine.

God, she was pitiful. She could just imagine how she'd react if he'd called her ma'am or some other cowboy cliché. She'd been on this job—as a police officer and now a D.A.'s investigator—for a long time now. Too long for a gesture like Nick Raymond's cowboy-hat tip to make her feel like a schoolgirl with a crush. She was cynical. She was strong. She was ambitious. And she was obviously in far too frail a mental state right now to deal with a sexy cowboy straight out of her starry-eyed preteen fantasies.

Seth better arrange for protection quickly, as he'd promised. She was in for a long couple of hours as it was.

She turned away and walked to a seating area near the side door and lowered herself to a bench. At least the bathroom was in an older section of the hospital, an area small and isolated, so she didn't have to worry about a lot of people going in and out. She tried to focus on the crowd filing into the main hospital entrance down the hall, rushing to visit relatives or have procedures, some with worry lines etched into their foreheads and some carrying balloons proclaiming that it was a girl. But try as she might, all she could think about was what had happened to Jimmy and how she was going to bring the scumbag who'd killed him to justice.

She'd lost track of time when she'd finally pulled her gaze from the stream of people and checked her watch. Nick and Jason had been in the restroom for more than fifteen minutes.

She pushed up from the bench and strode into the hall leading to the men's room, her heels echoing in the quieter part of the hospital. She stepped to the doorway and pushed the door open a crack, careful not to look inside. "Nick? Nick Raymond? Are you okay?"

No answer.

He had to be all right. She'd been sitting on the bench right outside the restroom hallway. This wasn't a busy area. No one suspicious had gone in or out. She would have seen them.

She pushed the door open wider. "Is anyone in here? Anyone at all?"

Again, no answer.

"I'm coming in." She shoved it open all the way and stepped inside.

The room was small, only two stalls flanked one wall and two urinals at different heights hung on the other. The yellow tile seemed of a long ago age, a sharp contrast with the more modern part of the hospital. The smell of disinfectant and strange sweet scent of pink urinal cakes tinted the air. And something else. A mixture of fresh air and exhaust from the street outside.

The ground-level window gaped wide open.

Chapter Three

"Mommy?" Jason yawned and squinted his eyes open, looking around the inside of the pickup and parking garage.

Pressure assaulted Nick's chest. He wondered if the four-year-old would wake when he transferred him into his car seat, but he wasn't ready for him to ask for his mother. He wasn't sure what to say. "I'm going to take you home, Jason."

"To Mommy?"

He couldn't lie to the kid, could he? "No. I'm sorry. Mommy won't be there." He stretched the belt across the booster seat and clicked it into place.

Jason nodded. "I'm not going to see Mommy anymore. She's dead."

The matter-of-fact way he stated it made Nick's heart ache. He had no idea what to say, what to do. He settled on giving the boy a nod.

"Will Melissa be at home?"

The D.A.'s investigator. "Melissa won't be there, either, Buddy."

"That's what Melissa calls me. Buddy."

"Oh."

"But you can call me Buddy, too."

"Okay. You can call me Daddy, if you want."

Jason just stared at him.

Guess he needed more of an explanation than that. "I'm your daddy, Jason. Remember what Melissa said?"

He nodded slowly, but his lower lip pushed out and started to tremble. "I want to see Melissa."

Distraction. Wasn't that what those parenting books he used to read suggested? The way to head off tears was with a distraction. "Look here. I have a movie for you to watch. Do you like movies?" He motioned to the DVD player.

The boy stared at it, lip still trembling. He raised his right hand to his head and tangled his fingers in his hair. His left thumb found his mouth. Tears swamped big blue eyes and rolled down his cheeks.

Nick blew out a breath. He couldn't spend time on this. He needed to get on the road, not sit here wrangling his son and waiting for Melissa, the police—or worse, the men who'd shot at his son before—to catch up. "I'm going to start the car and get the movie rolling." He closed the back door of the king cab and circled the bed. Somewhere in the city a siren screamed.

He opened the door and climbed behind the wheel. After starting the truck and the movie, he exited the parking structure.

He half expected the street to be barred by police cars, but traffic flowed freely up and down the boulevard. He could see police barricades still in place in front of the hotel two and a half blocks down. But other than that, the world went on as if nothing had changed.

Of course he had only to look into his rearview mirror at the little boy, one thumb in mouth, twirling his hair with his other hand, mesmerized by the mini DVD screen to remind himself *everything* had changed. He wasn't alone any longer. He had a son to protect. And he was damn well going to do it.

He pressed the gas and pulled out into traffic. The light ahead changed from green to yellow. The car in front of him slowed. Normally he might hit the gas hard, swerve into the open lane beside him and blast through the light before it switched to red. Maybe he should have now—every second on the street was exposing him to police, maybe even to men with guns—but instead he braked to a stop. Things were different. There was a child in the back.

And as he came to a halt behind the car stopped at the thick white line, he saw Melissa standing on the corner.

Oh, hell.

She started across the street with the other pedestrians hurrying to their cars or home after a long workday. She was going to walk right by them. She was going to see them. And then what was he going to do?

He looked in the rearview mirror. Cars filled the space behind him. He looked ahead and to the right. Turn. He had to turn before she reached him.

A crowd of people stepped off the curb, blocking his only escape route. They filed across the street, more people straggling behind them. Melissa came closer. She marched as if on a mission. A mission to find him and Jason, no doubt. She looked straight ahead, her sleek, blond hair blowing back from her cheeks.

Realizing he was holding his breath, he let it out and scooped another in. Drawing to the middle of the boulevard, she still hadn't spotted them. He leaned forward as if to urge the pedestrians to clear the crosswalk. He willed the light to change to green.

She drew even with the right bumper of the car in front of him, still missing him, still looking straight ahead. She crossed in front and stepped up onto the curb.

The light changed to green. One second passed. Two. The cars to the side started to move.

"Go," Nick said to the car ahead. "Come on."

The car inched forward.

On the curb, Melissa Anderson slowed her steps and glanced back over her shoulder.

Her eyes met Nick's.

There he was.

Melissa stopped in midstride, latching on to Nick Raymond's hazel gaze. His truck was already moving. Inching forward, nearly on the bumper of the sedan ahead of him. She couldn't catch him. Not unless she planned to race out into traffic and throw herself into the bed of his moving truck. Not likely.

But her car was parked nearby.

She raced down the sidewalk, clawing at the pocket in her bag for her keys, her silver hybrid already in her sights. Traffic moved slowly this time of day. He wouldn't be able to get too far ahead. She might be able to catch him before he reached the interstate, be nearby when he stopped for gas.

At least she had to try.

She hit the unlock button on her key remote and squeezed by the edge of traffic to the driver's door of her car. She slipped inside and jammed the key into the ignition. The car revved to life. She flicked on her blinker and eased into traffic.

Craning her neck, she scanned through three lanes of dark-colored sedans, delivery trucks and compacts, searching for a glimpse of Nick's truck. Once he left the state, it would be difficult to force him back to Denver. And she doubted he'd return voluntarily. Not after what happened this morning.

But if she wanted to help nail whoever shot Jimmy, she needed Nick. She'd been busy keeping Jason safe. She hadn't seen the men in the car. But Nick had. He was worried about keeping his son safe, but he was the one who needed protection.

Of course, she hadn't thought much about how she was going to provide it, since he obviously wasn't interested. As the D.A.'s investigator, she had all the powers of a county detective, including the power to arrest. With one call to Seth Wallace, she could get a material witness warrant for Nick. But the thought of putting him and his son through an arrest didn't feel right. If he forced her hand, she'd do it. For justice's sake. For Jimmy. But she'd rather not go that far.

Up ahead on the ramp leading onto I-25, she spotted a pickup that looked like Nick's. She followed the traffic flow. Merging onto the interstate, she hit the gas. The drive-time traffic had prevented Nick from getting too far ahead, but she still had a lot of ground to make up. If he pulled off to stop for gas or take a smaller highway, she wanted to be close enough to know it.

The miles ticked by. The number of cars dwindled. After they streamed past the outskirts of Denver, signs of city started to fade. The interstate took a wide bend, and she again spotted the pickup. She was closer now. Close enough to get a look at the Wyoming license plate with its picture of a cowboy on a bucking horse. The shadow of a booster seat peeked through the king cab's back window.

It was Nick Raymond, all right.

He hadn't stopped for gas since they'd left Denver. That truck was built for hauling, not for good mileage. He'd have to stop soon. At least he would provided he hadn't filled his tank when he'd arrived in Denver this morning.

The truck veered off the interstate and onto a highway heading for Laramie. Melissa followed. In Denver, she'd found comfort in knowing the roads and landscape better than Nick. Here the tables had turned. They were entering his home turf now, and the only navigational tool she had was the highway atlas she had tucked in under her front passenger's seat.

Funny, she'd always meant to get a GPS. Unfortunately the money always seemed to go for other things.

She pressed the gas pedal. As long as she could stay within sight of the pickup, she was fine. Not much of a challenge anymore, considering that Nick's truck, her car and a car behind her seemed to be the only vehicles on the highway.

He had to see her. She couldn't help wonder what he was thinking.

She glanced in the rearview, sizing up the dark blue sedan behind her. A blue sedan. Like the one outside the hotel this morning, the one that had fired on them and killed Jimmy.

A tremor lodged in the center of her chest. She glanced in the mirror again as long as she dared on the twisting mountain road. Evening had fallen on the drive and the darkness made it tough to see more than the outline of a driver and passenger and probably one other in the backseat. It couldn't be the car from this morning. Could it? It had to be her overactive imagination.

Her palms broke out in a sweat. She adjusted her grip on the wheel. Could they have noted the spot where Nick had parked his truck before walking to the hotel to pick up his son? Could they have waited all day, biding their time, hoping he'd return and give them a chance to remove the only witness to their drive-by?

Seth Wallace had feared something like this might happen. He'd wanted to take Nick into custody for his protection. She'd talked him out of it, told him to let her whisk the rancher and his son off to a hotel, keep them safe. And now…

She punched the button on the steering wheel, activating her phone. "No signal available," the flat voice intoned. She tried again. Same response. The mountains. They were already blocking cell phone signals. And they had a long way to go before they'd be in the clear.

She scooped in a deep breath. She had to stay calm. There were a lot of dark-colored sedans in the world.

And she wasn't sure, but the car behind them looked like it had only two people inside, not four. This might not be the shooter. This whole situation might just be in her mind.

She followed the winding highway, focusing on Nick's pickup ahead. She tried the phone again and again with no luck. The only sound was the hiss of tires on pavement, and the rapid thump of her pulse. The area around them was growing more remote with every mile that rolled under her tires. Soon night had fallen, the sky dark except for a glow of twilight beyond shadows of mountains. Even though it wasn't yet October, a dry powdery snow dusted the road.

A crack split the air like snapping ice.

Was that—

She looked in the rearview mirror. Behind her, the passenger window of the sedan was lowered. A head poked outside, a youngish face, short dark hair whipped by the wind. He had something in a tattoo-marked hand, and although she couldn't really see what it was, she didn't have to. She knew.

Another shot exploded.

The back window of Nick's truck shattered.

Melissa gripped the wheel, shock shuddering through her. *Oh, God. Oh, God. Jason.*

Ahead the pickup swerved, but stayed on the road.

She couldn't let them get off another round. She wouldn't. She had to stop them, whatever it took.

Taking a deep breath, she stomped on the brake. Her car skidded and started to spin.

Chapter Four

"You okay, Buddy? You okay, buddy?" Nick glanced into the backseat. He knew it was risky. The mountain highway twisted and wound like a snake. A missed turn and they could crash through the guardrail and find themselves plunging into the black ravine. But he had to know if his son was hurt. If Jason wasn't okay, nothing mattered.

A little hiccup rose from the backseat. A couple of breaths and it turned to a frightened little boy cry.

Headlights behind veered to the side.

Nick stole a glance in the rearview mirror. The little silver toy he'd guessed was Melissa's car spun on the slick mountain road. A smack shuddered through the air, the sickening crunch of metal on metal.

Oh, God.

Cars bounced off one another. One skidded toward the guardrail.

Nick brought his eyes back to the road in front of him. Lifting his foot from the gas, he slowed for the sharp turn ahead.

Another crash shuddered from behind. Melissa? The other car? He pulled in a shallow breath, then another.

Completing the turn, he piloted the truck up the switchback and looked down at the road below.

One car rested on the narrow shoulder, its beams shining out into blackness. Next to it, the guardrail gaped, wood and steel ripped away and cast down the mountainside.

The other car was nowhere to be seen.

Nick turned away from the wreckage. He slowed the truck and guided off onto an overlook, mind racing through what had just happened. The gunfire. Melissa's car skidding. The first crash and then one vehicle sailing through the rail.

The car that was left looked like Melissa's. Didn't it? Silver in color. Smaller in size. It had to be hers. A shudder gripped him. Why had she spun out of control in the first place? He'd only heard two gunshots, one had shattered his back window, and the other? Could it have hit her? Could Melissa be shot?

Safely stopping the car, he switched on the dome light and twisted in his seat to examine his son. Thumb planted in mouth, Jason was still sobbing, tears spilling from his big blue eyes and down plump cheeks in heartbreaking waves. But as far as Nick could tell, he hadn't been hurt. Not physically. Pebbled glass littered the backseat, glistening in the light.

"It's okay, Buddy." He unhooked the little guy's belt and helped him into the front. Gathering him into his arms, he checked him over again, just to be sure. He found nothing. Except for more emotional trauma, which Jason certainly didn't need, the little guy was unscathed. "It's okay, Buddy. It's all over. We're safe."

Rubbing his hand on the little shoulder, Nick peered

down off the overlook. The car's beams still gleamed out into nothingness, its nose caught on the edge of the crumpled guardrail. But now a woman stood on the pavement outside the car.

Melissa. Thank God.

Checking her cell phone, she circled the back of the car, as if assessing whether she could drive away. Even from this distance, Nick could see she wasn't going anywhere.

Nick brought his focus back to the truck's interior. Nick cleared as much pebbled glass from the back as he could and taped a sheet of plastic over the open stretch where the back window should be. After dumping tempered glass from the car seat, he strapped Jason back in. Settling back behind the wheel, he pulled out onto the road and headed down the switchback in the opposite direction.

He could see the controlled look on Melissa's face before he stopped the truck. The same look she'd had after the drive-by shooting this morning. He lowered the passenger window. "Get in." He gestured to his truck with the flip of a hand.

"No. I...I can't." She paused for a moment, then turned her back to him and peered down into the darkness.

He got out of the truck. Circling to the passenger side, he followed her line of sight. Tiny pinpricks of light beamed deep in the ravine's shadow. No one could have survived that kind of fall.

"I need to stay until help arrives."

"No. You don't."

She looked up at him. "You don't understand. I hit

the brakes…I did it on purpose…" She brought her hand to her forehead.

He understood perfectly what had happened. She was the one who didn't understand. "You can stay here all night, but you'll never get cell phone reception on this stretch of highway."

She shook her head. "It's my fault, I ki—"

"You saved our lives."

She looked at him through mussed bangs, as if she hadn't thought of it that way.

"You did. Thank you. Now let us help you. Get in the truck."

She didn't move. Instead, she glanced back at the car deep in the gully.

"I'm sorry," he said, making his voice softer. All he could think about was the fact that those men had shot out the back window. They'd come far too close to hurting Jason. He was just glad it was over and his little boy was safe. He didn't give a rat's ass what had happened to them as a result. But Melissa, she'd caused their crash. He could understand how she could be questioning herself now. "We'll call when we get out of the mountains. I promise. Now, come on. Jason is scared. He needs a familiar face."

She met his eyes. He could almost see her emotions shuffle into place, like a bird smoothing its feathers. She gave a nod and strode to the car.

She opened the back door of the king cab and climbed into the seat beside Jason. "I'm going to ride back here, if that's all right," she said.

"Of course." Nick slipped behind the wheel, started the truck and pulled back onto the highway. Miles rolled under the tires, twisting through the mountains, flattening briefly, then twisting again. Murmurs rose from the backseat, then settled into silence. He glanced into the rearview mirror to see Jason slumping to the side in his car seat. Melissa stared out the window into the darkness with shell-shocked eyes. But as vulnerable as her eyes made her appear, the rock-hard set to her chin seemed determined to meet whatever came next.

Nick never thought of himself as the nurturing type, but at that moment, he wanted nothing more than to make everything okay for his son and the woman who had saved Jason's life twice in one day. Whether she would let him was another story. But it was what she would do after she recovered that worried him most.

Because there wasn't a chance in hell he and Jason were returning to Denver, and he had a feeling she hadn't followed him just for sport.

MELISSA DIDN'T KNOW WHEN she'd fallen asleep or how long she'd been out, but when she awoke, total darkness still surrounded the truck and there wasn't a prick of light to be seen save for the stars overhead.

So this was what the middle of nowhere looked like at night.

She eyed Nick. From the backseat, she could see nothing but the silhouette of his hat against the dash's green glow. Even the rearview mirror didn't give her more than a glimpse of hat brim and a touch of wavy dark hair.

She turned her attention to his son sleeping in the car seat next to her. Jason's thumb was jammed in his open mouth, his free hand twined in the waves on the crown of his head, the only hair long enough for him to get a good hold.

The events of the day hit her with a rush that stole the oxygen from the truck's cab. Jimmy dead. Essie on life support. Jason and his father almost killed on the highway. The car at the bottom of the ravine.

She knew what Nick had said was correct—she'd saved his and Jason's lives. That's what she'd set out to do. But she'd also caused the deaths of whomever was in that car, and that fact vibrated deep in her chest like the echoes of an explosion.

The truck slowed. Nick turned off the highway and onto a side road. Gravel crackled under the tires. Logs of lodgepole pine framed each side of the gravel drive and stretched over the top. A metal sign hung from the top span, a cutout of a J inside a circle, like a cattle brand. Barbed wire gleamed in the headlight beams, stretching out on either side of the gateway. They drove under the sign, tires bumping over a cattle guard in the road.

"You awake?" Nick's voice rumbled through the cab.

How long had he been watching her?

She fought the urge to shrink back against the seat and wrap her arms over her chest. Or worse, start shaking and babbling like she had at the ravine. Straightening her back, she smoothed her lips into an expression more than one man had described as unreadable. None had meant it as a compliment, but she took it that way all the same. "What time is it?"

"Almost 4:00 a.m."

"I apologize for falling asleep like that. I should have kept you company."

"You needed the rest."

She didn't like the fact that he seemed to know how much. That he could have been watching her sleep, and she'd never know. "We need to call the authorities."

"Already did."

He'd made the call? She sat straight up in the seat. "Why didn't you wake me?"

"Like I said, you needed the rest."

She shook her head. "I needed to talk to the sheriff." She didn't even know in what county the crash had taken place. She rummaged under the seat. Touching the soft leather of her bag, she hauled it out, unzipped it and started fishing for her cell phone.

"Don't bother. There's no signal around here."

She found her phone and checked the readout. He wasn't lying. "Isn't there *any* cell phone service in Wyoming?"

"There is. Just not around here."

"Well I need to get somewhere that has service. I have to let the authorities know what happened."

"I already told them."

"That's not the same thing."

"It will have to do. At least for now."

Nick slowed the truck. Ahead a handful of lights peppered the dark slope in front of the truck. The hulks of buildings took shape. A collection of small cabins. A barn that looked like it came straight out of the Old West.

She tore her eyes from the cabins and focused on what had to be the main house. Although it, too, was built with logs, this place was bigger and fancier than any log cabin she'd ever seen. Constructed in multiple levels, the house boasted creative angles and railed decks. Generous windows overlooked the mountain landscape. "This is your ranch?"

His cowboy hat tilted forward in a nod. "It's a guest ranch. The bulk of the tourist season is over and I don't have any hunters booked until next week, so you have your pick of the cabins." He piloted the truck to a small parking area just to the west of the house and brought it to a halt.

"A guest ranch, huh, then you must have phone service." She glanced around. A faint light touched the eastern edge of the sky. The first glow of dawn.

"That's part of the charm of this place. People come here to escape the outside world."

She didn't believe it. "How do you take reservations?"

He threw an arm over the back of the passenger seat next to him and twisted to look her in the eye. "If you want to talk about this, let's step outside." His gaze flicked over Jason, still fast asleep.

Melissa nodded. As urgent as it was for her to get to a phone, she didn't want to wake the boy with an argument. He'd been through more than any kid should ever have to go through in his entire life. She didn't want to add to his trauma. She opened her door and stepped out into the bracing night air.

Nick followed, and they both quietly closed the doors behind them.

Melissa looked up at the cowboy. Face shadowed by his hat brim, she could read little of his expression, but the straight jaunt of his spine and the casual way he shifted his weight onto one boot clearly conveyed how comfortably in control of the situation he felt.

She stretched to her full height, wishing she'd worn higher heels. "How do you run a business like this without a phone?"

"I have a service that takes care of reservations."

She shook her head. "And if some rich client has a heart attack, do you send out the pony express to bring back an ambulance or do you prefer using passenger pigeons?"

The corners of his lips tilted upward. His shoulders jerked in a shrug. The movement was too abrupt, as if he was indeed hiding something.

And she had a guess as to what. "You have a satellite phone."

He didn't respond.

"I have to use it right away."

"No, you don't."

"I have to—"

He held up a hand. "The authorities are taking care of the sedan at the bottom of the ravine and your car, too. I'll arrange for you to get back to Denver, I promise, but first I need to get something clear."

"What?"

"I need to know why you were following me."

"What do you mean?"

"We are not going back to Denver."

She figured they'd get around to this argument sooner rather than later. "Most witnesses who need protection can't get it."

"Feel free to give them ours. Now that we're back at the Circle J, I have it under control."

"You might feel like you're hiding from the outside world, but there's nothing to keep the outside world from finding you. Even in the middle of nowhere." She gestured at the darkness around them. No, not darkness. Now that she was outside of the car, the sky seemed to be alive with more stars than she'd seen in her lifetime. Add the creep of dawn, pink along the horizon, and this place looked far from nowhere. It was isolated, sure, but it was definitely a somewhere. And a beautiful somewhere at that.

"Isn't Jason a bit young to testify in court?"

A heaviness settled into her chest. She'd wanted to explain it all to Nick at the hospital, allay his fears for his son, but Seth and Cory Calhoun had talked her into holding back. All they had was a theory. No facts to back it up that she knew of, not yet. But in light of all that had happened since, she wasn't going to hold back any longer. "Yes. A four-year-old's testimony has limited value. And we're pretty sure he didn't see the actual murder."

"Then why do you need him in Denver?"

"We don't. We need you."

He took a step back and stared at her as if she were speaking another language. "So Jason isn't much of a witness at all? Then why the drive-by outside the hotel?"

"They…" She paused, still not sure if she really wanted to believe the theory Seth sprang on her in the hospital, although it was better than someone gunning for a four-year-old kid. She swallowed into a tight throat. "We don't think Jason was the target. We think Jimmy was."

Nick tilted his head to the side. "Who's we?"

"Seth, Detective Marris, and another D.A.'s investigator, Cory Calhoun."

"The men who were arguing in the hospital corridor."

"Yes."

"So Jason was just in the wrong place at the wrong time?"

"Not exactly. Calhoun thinks Jimmy was targeted because he was the lead detective on your ex-wife's case." She paused, wishing that was all. "And somehow the shooters knew just when Jimmy would be bringing Jason to the police station. They were in position, waiting."

"That's what I saw." He tilted his head to the side. "You think someone told them. Who?"

Possible explanations had been hanging on the edges of Melissa's mind since she'd talked to Seth at the hospital. But out of all the people who could have known their plan to bring Jason to the police station that morning, she *really* didn't want to believe any could have sold him out like that. "We don't know. But we're going to find out."

"And the men shooting at our truck? It looked like the same car."

She nodded. The description he'd given at the crime scene had matched the car that crashed into the ravine to a *T*. "You saw them murder a police detective."

He turned away from her and paced a few feet, shaking his head. Taking a deep breath, he looked back in her direction. This time one of the lights on the house's exterior caught the side of his face. He looked tired and more stressed than his body language had suggested. "I talked to a police artist at the hospital. Can't they just use those sketches to identify the bodies? If it's even possible."

"You said you saw four men in that car in Denver."

"That's right."

"It didn't look like there were any more than two last night."

"Two? It was dark and everything was happening way too fast. How can you know that?"

"I saw two men. I'm sure." When it had happened, it had been dark, and she hadn't been sure. But she wasn't going to let him assume he was off the hook.

He let out a sigh, as if he was getting tired of the whole argument. "I'm not going back."

"How can you say that? The men who murdered Jimmy might still be out there. If you don't care about Jimmy, and you don't care that they're likely tied to your ex-wife's murder in some way, then you should at least care that they almost shot your son."

He frowned. "Seems if I went back, I'd be inviting them to take another try."

She couldn't believe what she was hearing. Nick Raymond seemed like a good guy. She'd even had visions of him as a hero in one of those Westerns Jimmy had loved to watch. What a joke. You could rely on a hero to do the right thing. You could rely on them to see things through. "So that's it? You don't care about justice?"

"Justice? Let me tell you about justice." He stepped forward.

Too close for her comfort. She took a step back.

"Justice is a man finally finding the child he had stolen from him three years ago." His voice boomed in the quiet night, not loud, but ringing with emotion. "Justice is a little boy who knows he's safe when he steps out the front door or rides in his daddy's truck. And right now, justice is you leaving us *alone.*"

She pulled in a shaky breath. He'd been through a lot. She had to remember that. "I'm sorry. I know this has been incredibly tough. It has been for all of us."

"Tomorrow I'll drive you to Jackson and you can rent a car to get back to the city." He took off his hat, raked a hand through his hair and replaced it. "You can find your justice, Melissa, but leave me to mine. Please."

She said nothing. She felt bad for him and ashamed she hadn't tried to see the situation from his point of view from the outset, but she wasn't ready to give up. Not yet.

She watched Jason through the side window. He was still sound asleep, slumped to the side in a way only a child's body could bend. She supposed she could threaten to arrest Nick. But she doubted a mere threat would work, and she still couldn't stand the thought of slapping on the cuffs. They weren't even in Colorado anymore, a detail that would surely complicate things. There had to be another way.

"Now do you want to pick out a cabin for the rest of tonight, or should I just give you one?" Nick said.

She looked up at the house. The place was huge. Surely he had an extra bedroom available, close enough for her to work on him, convince him returning to Denver was necessary. Close enough…

She almost laughed at the direction her thoughts had led back in the hospital, before Nick had tricked her and slipped away. She wasn't some weak, pitiful thing with a cowboy fetish. She would never be that woman. She could handle being within the same walls as Nick Raymond. And she would get him back to Denver. Somehow.

She folded her arms across her chest. "I'd like to stay near Jason, at least for tonight. I want to make sure he's okay."

Nick's gaze flicked to the truck's interior, then back to Melissa. He didn't speak for what seemed like forever, as if sizing up her sincerity. Finally he gave a nod, his hat brim tilting low. "I think that would probably help."

She met his words with a smile despite herself. She'd worked with kids before, and she was good at relating to them. That was why she often worked on cases involving children. But Jason was different. She wasn't sure if it was the kid himself or his parallels to her own childhood, but he'd wedged himself close to her heart. "Thanks."

"I got to warn you, if you think you can talk me into going back to Denver, you're fooling yourself." Nick's voice was gentle, even though his words called her out. He lifted his hand to his hat and gave it a slight tip. "But it'll be nice to have a woman in the house all the same."

Somewhere deep inside, Melissa felt a weak flutter, and she had to wonder if she'd just made a big mistake.

Chapter Five

"Mommy always has grape." Jason stuck out his lower lip.

Nick glanced down at the piece of toast. He'd thought for sure Jason would like toast with strawberry jam. It was almost noon, and they had yet to eat breakfast. The little hellion had already refused eggs and bacon, but Nick had hoped he'd solved the problem with toast. "Sorry. Strawberry is all I have. How about honey?"

"Mommy gives me grape."

Nick couldn't help but wonder how much of the refusal to eat had to do with jam and how much had to do with losing his mother. "Oatmeal? How about that?"

Jason shook his head. "Mommy didn't like oatmeal."

Nick remembered that. He remembered a lot of other things Jason's mommy didn't like. Like the ranch. Like the ranching life. Like him.

"Should we just skip breakfast for now and go see the horses?" Nick flinched at the hint of desperation in his voice. Not good. If Jason picked up on how much he wanted him to fall in love with the Circle J, he'd hate it as much as he hated strawberry jam.

"Actually, I want to see Melissa."

Actually? Nick didn't realize kids that young used words so big. He stifled a smile. "Melissa didn't get much sleep last night, buddy. I think she's still snoozing."

"I'm awake."

Her voice came from behind him. He turned in time to see her step into the kitchen.

Her skin glowed. Her face seemed younger and more real without makeup. She was wearing the same clothes she had on yesterday, except for the jacket. But where most people would be a bit rumpled around the edges, she looked fresh, like she hadn't slept in the clothes at all.

Maybe she hadn't.

He shook his head and thrust to his feet. Walking into the kitchen, he carefully steered around the image in his mind and gestured to the space around them. "What do you think of the place?"

She scanned the big, country-style kitchen, the adjoining dining hall and the great room beyond. Her eyes stopped at the fireplace and the elk rack above the mantle. "Looks cozy, like a real Western lodge. I can see why people like to stay here."

"I'm going to ride on a horse." Jason threw out his skinny little chest, as if suddenly bursting with pride.

"That sounds fun."

"You can come, too."

Melissa glanced at Nick. "I think your dad wants to—"

"Of course you can come. I have plenty of horses." He didn't know where the invitation had sprung from, but there it was, jumping from his mouth. Of course, the thought of her sleeping naked between the sheets of one of the guest rooms could have him agreeing to just about anything.

She held out her arms, showing off her white blouse and trousers. "I'm not exactly dressed for it."

Nick glanced at his son. The little guy hung on every word from Melissa's lips. Obviously he'd grown close to her in the short time since his mother had died. He was used to being without a father. But he obviously needed a mother figure. So badly it made Nick's chest hurt if he dwelled on it too much. "If you can get him to eat some breakfast, and have some yourself, I'll see if I can fix the clothing problem."

She shared a smile with Jason. "You're on."

Nick ran upstairs and let himself into the attic. Winding through stacks of items in storage, he found the box he was looking for. Hefting it in one arm, he carried it down to the kitchen.

By the time he returned, Melissa was sitting next to Jason at the table. She bit into a piece of toast, and Jason did the same. She had made herself at home at the stove and served up a plate of scrambled eggs to Jason, too.

She picked up her fork. "Don't forget your egg." She took a bite from her own plate, and the four-year-old stuffed a forkful into his mouth without complaint.

Amazing.

She took a sip of coffee and eyed the box. "Old clothes?"

He opened the cardboard flaps and pulled out a pair of women's Wranglers. He draped them on a vacant chair. He followed with a Western-style, button-down shirt and a pair of Tony Lama boots, hardly worn. "I hope these are the right size."

She finished her eggs, then checked the labels. "They should work. Your wife's?"

He nodded, resisting the urge to remind her about the *ex* part. "If you want to put them on, we'll meet you down here when you're ready."

She threw the clothes over her forearm and gathered the boots. Halfway down the hall that led to the stairs, she stopped and turned back to face him. "I need to talk to you."

He'd known that was coming. "I told you last night. I made the calls. Everything is being taken care of. Other than that, we don't have much to talk about."

"I need to make some calls myself." She eyed him, somehow looking both firm, as she had the night before, and softer than he expected.

"Later."

She nodded, but she didn't look satisfied.

If she was going to lobby him about returning to Denver, about identifying bodies, about doing his part for justice, he wasn't going to give her the chance. "I promised Jason we'd ride horses. Everything else will have to wait. Please."

She looked past him, smiling at Jason who was finishing his last morsels of egg. "Of course."

"So we'll meet you back down here?" he prodded.

She gave him a reluctant nod and headed up the steps.

Avoiding this argument might be tougher than he thought. But he wasn't going to give in. He deserved a moment with his son, and damn it, he was going to take it. Whether Melissa Anderson agreed or not.

He had breakfast dishes cleared and Jason washed up and ready to go when he heard footsteps coming back down the stairs. He turned around as Melissa made her entrance into the dining room.

His throat went dry.

He hadn't thought much about lending her Gayle's old clothes. God knew, she'd hardly worn them when she lived here. And she certainly hadn't thought enough of the jeans and boots to take them with her when she ran off to the city. As far as he was concerned, Gayle had rejected them right along with the ranch and him. But seeing Melissa dressed in those same clothes made him realize how much like Gayle she really looked with her sleek blond hair. Hell, how much like Gayle she *was*, with her efficient, businesslike manner and the righteous ambition that made her eyes spark like a warrior's when she was trying to get her way.

And here he'd invited her right into the main house, set her up as a mother figure for Jason and dressed her for the part like he was trying to rewrite history.

He needed to have a long talk with a shrink.

"What's wrong?"

"Nothing. Let's go." He grabbed the door knob and yanked it open, the realization of what he'd done ringing through his body like some kind of morning alarm he'd finally awakened enough to hear.

WHAT WAS SHE DOING ON this beast's back?

Melissa resisted the urge to drop the reins and grab the saddle horn with both hands. The horse veered from one side of the pen to the other, not the direction she had in mind.

"Sit back in the saddle and raise your rein hand." Nick stood on the ground, the lead rope in his hand controlling the horse Jason rode.

She did what he said, but the horse didn't seem to notice, he just kept walking wherever he pleased. This was not working. She couldn't stand being this out of control, this inept.

The only thing worse about this experience had been Nick teaching her how to saddle the animal. The procedure itself wasn't that hard, but having him standing so close behind her she could feel his body heat had been uncomfortable at best. And when he'd cupped her hands in his, helping her move the straps into place….

She shook her head and focused on preventing her horse from plowing through the fence and joining the small herd on the other side. "He won't listen to anything I tell him. What am I doing wrong?" She cringed at the helpless shrill of her own voice.

Leading Jason's perfectly calm horse up next to hers, Nick frowned up at her. "You're not taking control."

She could have told him that. "So how do I take control?"

"You set your mind to it."

"It's that easy, huh?"

"No. But it's a start. Think about how you feel when you're driving in busy traffic."

She could do that. "The problem is, I don't know where the gas pedal is. And the brake. And I obviously have absolutely no clue where to find the steering wheel."

"We went over all those things. Legs, weight, hand."

He was right. He'd explained how she squeezed the horse with her legs to get him to move forward, shifted her weight back and raised her rein hand to stop him, and moved her hand from side to side, neck reining him to turn. "Then why can't I get those things to work?"

"You're not setting your mind to what you want."

"Setting my mind to what I want?" She had no idea what he was talking about.

"I'll bet in your world, you're good at setting your mind to what you want, aren't you?"

"I suppose." In her world, she identified what she wanted, and she set about getting it. She wasn't one of those women who relied on others to do it for her. Not like her mother had been. "But that's not the same thing."

"Actually it is. The horse is reading the signals you're sending him. Those signals aren't making sense because you're not thinking about what you want, you're thinking about the mechanics of riding."

"So I need to think about the fact that I want to go over there." She nodded at the gate on the far side of the pen.

"Yes. When you're driving in traffic, you focus on getting from here to there. You signal, you press down on the gas, you move the steering wheel this way and that, but you don't concentrate on all those little things to the point where you're not concentrating on your goal."

"But that's what I'm doing when I ride."

"Exactly."

"Got it." At least she thought she did. She took in a deep breath of heady mountain air and focused on the gate. *I want to go to that gate. I want to go to that gate.* She slid her reins to the left, moving the horse off the fence. She pressed her legs against his sides. And miracle upon miracles, he stepped forward. She kept her focus glued to the gate and in no time, her mount had crossed the arena. She raised her hand and sat back in the saddle, and the gelding stopped in front of the gate.

"See?" Nick said.

A warm rush flowed through her body. She could do this. She could take control. And the most amazing thing was how pure the victory was, unlike the challenges she faced in her job. Animals responded in an honest way. They took advantage if you let them, but they followed if you took the lead. As long as you didn't let them down, they didn't let you down.

Amazing.

She could see why people vacationed at a ranch to escape reality and fill themselves with that rush of simple accomplishment, of control. She could see how a life like this could become addicting. And even though this brief interlude didn't change what she needed to do, she was glad Nick had forced her to take the time to do it.

The afternoon stretched on with more riding followed by unsaddling and cleaning up the horses, helping the ranch hands clean the barn. By the time Melissa walked side by side back to the house with Nick and Jason, she was feeling as fulfilled and exhausted as the four-year-old holding her hand.

A brown delivery truck parked in front of the house. The driver hefted a box out of the back and carried it to the front porch. There he stacked it with three other boxes already there.

"What the hell?" Nick said under his breath.

Melissa eyed him. "Not expecting anything?"

He didn't answer, just lengthened his stride.

Strange. Melissa was so used to ordering things online and seeing delivery trucks buzzing around Denver that she hadn't thought twice. But apparently, a delivery truck sighting was a rare thing on the Circle J Ranch.

They reached the truck and Nick flagged down the driver before he could pull yet another box from the back of the truck. "What's all this?"

"Delivery from Denver."

Melissa tensed.

Nick glanced at her, then back to the driver. "Who is it from?"

He shrugged a burly shoulder. "You Nick Raymond?"

"Yes."

"I need you to sign for it." The driver motioned to Nick to follow and circled to the front of the truck.

As he pulled out his clipboard to make it all official, Melissa and Jason climbed the steps to the porch. Melissa paused when she reached the boxes. Leaning down, she focused on the return address. A shiver of recognition ran down her spine. She turned to find Nick climbing the porch steps. "I have to call my office."

He let out a heavy breath. "How about I drive you to Jackson after we get a late lunch? You can get cell service and a car rental there and be on your way back to Denver tonight, if you like."

And out of his hair? She held up her hands in front of her, palms out. "No. Not yet. I have to make a call first."

"Now you want to stay?"

"I need to talk to Seth. And I will have to take these boxes with me."

He looked at her like he thought she might be half-crazy. "Come again?"

She glanced back at the address, just to make sure. She was right. This could be important. Very important. "Do you recognize the return address?"

He peered down at the printed label. When he brought his gaze back to her, he looked more confused than ever. "Who sent them?"

She took a deep breath, wishing she had a way to lessen the impact of what she was about to say. "Your wife."

Chapter Six

"Ex," he said automatically. He felt dizzy, his mind whirring with what Melissa had just said. Gayle had sent boxes? After all these years, why would Gayle send him boxes?

"And the date they were picked up…" She trailed off.

He looked down at the date printed on one of the boxes. It held no significance to him, but he had a bad feeling he could guess what the date meant. "What about it?"

"It's the day." She glanced at Jason.

She didn't have to elaborate about what day she meant. The boxes had been picked up the day Gayle was murdered.

His pulse increased its pace, thrumming in his ears. He glanced at his son. The boy looked tired. After all they'd been through yesterday, little sleep last night, and their active adventure today, surely he'd need a nap. And now was the right time. "Hey buddy, let's get something to eat and take a nap. How about it?"

Jason shot him a frown. He set his little chin in a clear sign of mutiny.

Whatever points Nick had earned with the horseback ride, he had a feeling he'd just lost them. He looked to Melissa.

She gave him a nod. "Hey Jason, come with me. Your daddy is going to make us lunch." Melissa held out her hand.

Jason gripped her fingers with his little ones, beaming as she led him inside.

Nick watched them disappear down the hall. He should have known mentioning the word *nap* wasn't a good idea. He just hadn't given it much thought. His mind was still careening with the idea that these boxes could have come from Gayle herself on the day she died.

He hauled the boxes into the den, then joined Melissa and Jason for what they were calling lunch, even though the stock would soon be looking for their evening feeding. Then while Melissa got the little guy settled in bed for his nap, Nick grabbed a box cutter and returned to the den.

He knelt beside the closest box and eyed the return address. After three years of nothing, no word, no call, not even a damned Christmas card, she sent him five boxes? None of it made sense. But then, Gayle had never made much sense to him. And even before she'd left, she had made it perfectly clear he never made sense to her.

Pressure assaulted his chest and tightened his throat. He wasn't in love with Gayle any longer. Her abandonment and all the time he'd devoted to trying to find his son had killed any feelings he'd had toward her. But seeing how dependent Jason was on Melissa just drove home how much the little guy had lost when his mother died. And even though the love he once had for Gayle was dead, she still had a tight hold on him. His attraction for Melissa was evidence of that.

He slipped the blade out from the box cutter's plastic handle.

"Wait."

He started slightly at the sound of her voice. He turned around to see Melissa standing in the doorway.

"Don't open them. I need to take these back to Denver sealed in case they contain some kind of evidence."

"Not a chance." Nick brought razor's edge against packing tape and slit. "I'm not going to Denver, and I want to know what Gayle sent."

Melissa stepped to his side for a better view.

He opened the cardboard flaps. Removing crumpled newspaper, he exposed a jumble of action figures and a tangle of Hot Wheels tracks. "Toys?" He opened another box. This one packed with Legos, Lincoln Logs and various stuffed animals. "Jason's, I would guess." Too bad he hadn't opened the boxes before the little guy fell asleep. He'd probably be thrilled to have his own toys back. But that was the only thing about this that Nick found clear. "Why would Gayle send Jason's toys?"

Melissa's eyebrows hunkered low over sharp eyes. "I wonder…"

"Wonder what?"

She shook her head. "If she was planning to move back here to the ranch. Or at least to send Jason."

He blew a laugh through his nostrils. "You're kidding, right? After all this time? Why would she do that?"

"To get him away from whatever was going on in Denver? To hide him? To keep him safe?"

Her theory hit him in the chest with the force of a well-aimed kick. *Could it be possible? Is that what this meant?*

He cut the tape of the third box and opened the cardboard flaps. Paper packed the box, some contained neatly in file folders, some loose. He fished out a package of snapshots of Jason as a baby. The only photos Gayle had sought fit to take when she'd left.

Melissa stepped to the couch and sat down beside him. Her scent drifted over him, something light and floral mixed with fresh air and a warm hint of horse.

He focused on the papers in the box. "Apparently she wanted to hide more than Jason."

She reached into the box, pulled out a folder and started sifting through the papers inside. "Financial records. Credit card bills. Utility bills."

"Why would she want to hide things like that?"

"It's hard to say. But credit cards could tell us where she was and what she was doing during certain time periods. That might be valuable."

He leaned forward to get a look at the credit card bills in her hands. "Those dates are a year old."

Melissa frowned and nodded toward the box. "See what else is in here."

He focused on the stack of Gayle's bills filling the box. "So what should I be looking for?"

"Anything unusual, anything with the name José Sanchez, any photos, bank and phone records, personal correspondence of any kind. If there's something here that can tie your ex-wife directly to Sanchez, that would be very helpful."

"José Sanchez. That's the guy."

Melissa nodded.

Somehow, having a name for the man who had killed Gayle didn't make him feel better. Neither did seeing the fake name she'd been using—Gayle Rogers—the reason the authorities and his private investigators hadn't been able to track her down. A heaviness bore down on his shoulders. He would have fought her for custody with everything he had. She knew that. Was that why she'd gone to such lengths to hide?

Unable to come up with an answer, he fished out a folder and opened it. "Credit card statements." He scanned line after line of charges for restaurants, fancy hotels, clothing boutiques and shoe stores. All the things Gayle loved and couldn't get on a ranch in Middle-of-Nowhere, Wyoming, as she used to call the Circle J. He flipped through month after month, noting other charges, too. Ones for tot karate, tot piano lessons and the educational children's toy stores that Gayle favored. All advantages Gayle wanted Jason to have, all things that were hard to come by around here without driving an hour or more. He flipped through the last of the statements and closed the folder.

"See anything unusual?"

"No." He set the folder on two Melissa had already scanned and reached for another. Records for Gayle's cell phone this time, lists of numbers there was no way for him to recognize, what seemed like an astronomical bill for the extra minutes she'd racked up, and little more. "You said you were interested in phone records?"

Melissa glanced up from the file folder she'd been looking through. "Yes." She reached out a hand.

He gave her the folder.

Eyebrows dipping low, she flipped through page after page. "I've seen her the records for her BlackBerry. Jimmy got a warrant for them. But this cell phone isn't even with the same company."

"You haven't seen these before?"

"I didn't even know she had a second cell phone."

Realizing he was watching her a little too closely, Nick pulled another file from the box, this one filled with year-to-date credit card bills. The expenditures themselves seemed much the same as the previous year.

"Huh."

Nick looked up. "What is it?"

Melissa frowned down at the cell phone records. "I don't know. This is weird."

"What is?" He hadn't seen anything weird, not that he'd recognize weirdness if it bit him, not where Gayle was concerned.

"This number...and she's called it over and over in the months leading up to her death." Her tone dipped. More than serious. Closer to shocked.

Whatever was going on, it couldn't be good. Pressure clamped down on the back of Nick's neck. "What number?" Nick braced himself for an answer he couldn't fathom but still wasn't sure he wanted to hear.

"My work number. Gayle was calling someone at the district attorney's office." She looked up from the paper, her eyes latching on to his. "I'm afraid this might be even more complicated than I thought."

MELISSA'S FINGERS trembled as she punched the number into Nick's satellite phone. When she saw her office's number on Gayle's bill, she hadn't known what to think. She still didn't. But she aimed to find out what was going on.

Seth picked up on the second ring. "Yeah."

She perched on the edge of the queen-size bed in her guest room. "It's Melissa."

"Melissa? Are you all right? Your car—"

"Was found in the mountains. I know. Have authorities identified the men in the sedan that went through the guardrail?"

"No. Mel—"

"Were they dead?"

"Yes."

"There were two of them, right?"

"Yes."

"Did you get the license—"

"Stop right there. What happened to you? Are you okay? Where are you? I've been trying to get in touch with you since I got the call about your car this morning."

Melissa pulled in a breath. Her relationship with Seth had always been all business from her first day on the job, and she liked those boundaries. But his concern for her well-being felt good all the same. "I'm fine. I'm in Wyoming."

"Wyoming?"

"At Nick Raymond's ranch." She peered out the

window. The sun had already sunk behind the mountains. Their shadows loomed against a sky still too bright to be considered twilight. She'd awakened so late, her day at the ranch seemed to be ending before it had really begun.

"Why the hell did you go all the way up there?"

"It wasn't my idea, trust me. But that's not why I'm calling."

"You're calling about Essie Castillo."

Essie. She hadn't even thought of Essie. "How is she?"

"You don't know then."

Heaviness weighed on her chest. A sob caught in her throat. She didn't have to ask. The tone of Seth's voice told her everything. But she forced the words out just the same. "Know what?"

"She didn't make it, Melissa. I'm sorry."

Melissa pushed back a flood of tears. She couldn't afford to give in to her feelings over Essie and Jimmy. Not yet. All she could do for them was find the men who killed them. That was what she had to focus on now.

"Are you okay?"

She willed her voice to sound less shaken than she felt. Seth's concern for her was sweet, but he would also use it as an excuse to take control. She'd always been careful not to show any weakness around him for just that reason. "I'm fine."

"Marris has turned Essie's life upside down and found nothing. The shooter's target had to be Jimmy Bernard."

Melissa nodded, although something illogical inside

her still resisted the idea that someone would want to kill Jimmy. She cleared her throat. "Seth, five boxes were delivered here. Gayle Rodgers sent them the day she died."

"You opened them." Not a question, but a statement. Obviously he could read her voice despite her efforts.

"I know. I should have left them sealed, brought them back." She could have blamed it all on Nick, saved herself, but she couldn't bring herself to do that. When it came down to it, she wanted to see what was in those boxes as much as he had.

"What was inside?"

"Most of them contained toys and kids books. I think she might have planned to bring Jason back to the ranch. Maybe to get away from some threat she felt."

"A threat?"

"It makes me doubt Sanchez's motive was simple robbery. I wonder if she knew him, if she felt some kind of pressure from him that she was looking to escape." The thought that Gayle might have gotten into drugs and Sanchez was her supplier had occurred to Melissa, even before this. But she had no real evidence.

"Interesting. But you found something else, too."

Again, it was as if he'd read between the words she'd said, and added up the ones she hadn't. "Papers. Financial stuff, credit card statements, that kind of thing."

"And there was something that caught your eye?"

"Records for a cell phone I've never seen before."

"And?"

"She made some calls, a lot of them, actually."

"To?"

"Our office."

Silence answered her.

"Why was Gayle Rodgers calling our office, Seth? And why didn't I know about this before?"

The faint sound of a heavy exhale rasped over the phone. "I didn't want you to find out this way."

"Find out what?" She wished she could read Seth like he could read her. "Tell me."

"Come back to Denver. Bring Raymond and the boy."

"What were you referring to, Seth? What didn't you want me to find out?"

"I can't tell you this over the phone, Melissa."

"Can't tell me or won't?"

"Won't."

She gripped the phone, hoping by holding on tight she could keep her hands from shaking along with her voice. "No good, Seth. I have to know what's happening. I'm not going to drag Nick and Jason back to Denver without understanding what's going on."

"Knowing and understanding are two different things."

"Tell me."

"If I tell you, you'll bring the cowboy and the boy back?"

"It depends. I have to be able to assure him they'll be safe." And convince Nick to do something he had insisted he wasn't going to do.

"And you think they're safe at Raymond's ranch?"

"Aren't they?" The tremor settled in her stomach.

"I don't know."

The fact that Seth would admit to not knowing something worried Melissa most of all. "Tell me what's going on, and I'll make sure they're safe."

"And?"

"And I'll talk Nick into returning to Denver."

"And if he refuses, you'll arrest his ass and drag him back."

She hesitated. Yesterday putting Nick and his son through that kind of trauma felt cruel and unnecessary. After the time they'd spent together today, it felt like a betrayal. "We've crossed state lines."

"Find a way to make it work. Raymond is a witness. Just do your job."

Her job. She nodded into the phone as if Seth could see her. Her job had shaped her life, made it possible for her to become who she wanted to be. Seth was right. She'd do her job and things would work out. Nick and Jason would stay safe. They would find Jimmy's killers. Justice would be done in the end. "Okay. I'll bring him back. We'll leave tomorrow. Now tell me what's going on."

"Gayle Rodgers was working with our office."

Melissa felt cold. Informants and witness worked with the district attorney's office every day. But the way Seth had tried to hold the information back, the way he'd built up to the revelation, she knew she wasn't going to like this one bit. "Working with us how? Why?"

"It was about Jimmy, Melissa."

She shook her head. "Jimmy? What do you mean, it was about Jimmy? What was about Jimmy?"

"He's been involved in some…things. Things we were looking into."

"What are you saying?"

"Jimmy Bernard was being investigated for taking bribes from the Latin Devils."

The name of José Sanchez's gang shuddered through her like a physical force.

"I'm sorry, Melissa. Gayle Rodgers was one of our informants."

"No. I don't believe you."

"I wouldn't make up something like this. You know that. I liked Jimmy. The idea of this hurts me as much as it hurts you, but the law is the law. We can't just turn our backs because we like someone. And cops have to be subject to the law the same as everyone else."

She leaned forward and rubbed her forehead. This was ridiculous. An outrageous lie. "Gayle Rodgers worked in a private law office. How would she even know Jimmy, let alone have anything to inform about?"

Silence answered on the other end.

"Seth?"

"We'll talk about that when you get here."

"Just tell me."

"We're still investigating. I'll fill you in when you get back to Denver."

"Investigating…" She closed her eyes. It was her job to further investigate the case against Sanchez, to shore up the weak spots. Although they had two pieces of physical evidence that tied him to the crime, both his fingerprints on the murder weapon—a heavy, brass statuette—and the victim's personal belongings in his possession, the case was weak when it came to motive. The court didn't require a motive for a conviction, but juries tended to like knowing why the crime was committed. And Sanchez never struck Melissa as the robbery type. "Are you revisiting Gayle's murder?"

"We're looking at everything."

"You're not. You can't be."

"Can't be what?"

"You can't be thinking that Jimmy killed Gayle to keep her quiet." The words sounded so preposterous she had to stifle a giggle. She felt like she was teetering on the edge of a stress-fueled laughing jag.

"No, we're thinking Sanchez killed Gayle to protect the arrangement with Jimmy."

"You're not kidding." She'd known he wasn't, but somewhere in the back of her mind, she'd still held out hope that all this was some kind of tasteless joke.

"Like I said, I don't want to believe it, either. And I'm not saying it's fact. That's why we're looking into it, being thorough, even now."

Even now that Jimmy was dead, he meant. "And who killed Jimmy?"

"He arrested Sanchez. Their deal was that he look the other way."

"The Latin Devils." And if the Devils killed Jimmy... "You think the gang is after Nick."

"Now you understand why I'm worried about keeping him safe?"

She understood. The gang had a reputation for brutality against anyone who crossed them. They might just follow Nick out of Denver to get rid of an eyewitness. But the rest? No way. Not for a second. "You'll show me the case against Jimmy in detail when I get back?"

"If it's what you want."

"It is." She wouldn't believe Jimmy Bernard was

dirty. She never would, no matter what the evidence. But if she could get a look at what they had against him, she could work on taking their case apart brick by brick.

She could clear Jimmy's name and give him the justice he deserved.

Chapter Seven

The sky outside was dark and Nick and Jason had already eaten a small supper and helped the ranch hands feed the horses by the time Melissa emerged from her room, his satellite phone in hand. "We need to go back to Denver."

He was afraid she'd say that. "You know my answer."

"Things have changed."

"How?"

She glanced in Jason's direction.

A Hot Wheels car in each hand, he made motor sounds with his lips, alternately driving the cars on their tracks and over the table's edge.

"How have things changed?" Nick repeated.

"It seems she was an informant."

Melissa hadn't specified who the *she* referred to, but she didn't have to. An informant. That was a new twist. "For the D.A.'s office?"

"Seth says they were looking into police corruption." She paused. Just as Nick was about to prod, she took a breath. "The D.A.'s office was investigating Jimmy."

She'd stated the name with little emotion, but Nick

wasn't fooled. He'd seen how broken up she'd been when Detective Barnard died. He'd sensed there was more between them than the fact that they worked together on a case here and there. "I'm sorry."

She waved his words away, but instead of continuing, she turned her head to the side.

Was she crying? It appeared so. He didn't want to pry into something so painful. And he wouldn't—if his and his son's lives weren't connected to this—but as it was, he needed to know. "This Jimmy, he was special to you, wasn't he?"

"Yes." She kept her face turned to the side and tilted her chin toward the ceiling, as if using gravity to keep the tears from breaking free.

"A lover?" His voice hung in the air, awkward and inappropriate even to his own ears. "I'm sorry. I know it's not my business. It's just—"

She shook her head. "It's okay. We weren't lovers. Nothing like that. Jimmy was more like the father I never had."

Nick had no reason to feel relieved, but he did all the same. He nodded in what he hoped was an understanding way. "I'm doubly sorry, then."

"Thanks." She dropped her gaze to the contents of the box. "Jimmy's the reason I got into police work."

A cop. She'd originally been a cop. He couldn't say he was surprised. The way she'd handled the shooting on the street and took out the car that was gunning for them on the mountain road seemed like the work of a cop. "How did you end up with the district attorney's office?"

She looked away from him, as if she was uncomfortable talking about herself. Or at least uncomfortable with his question. "I started as a police officer for the city. There were more opportunities for advancement working for the county, at least at that time, so I switched."

Opportunity for advancement. The unease he'd felt earlier clamped down on the back of his neck. Ambition. Another uncomfortable parallel with Gayle. This attraction of his...he really was replaying the past. At least now that he recognized it, he could steer clear. "I'm sorry you had to find this out about your mentor, but I don't understand what it has to do with us returning to Denver."

"He wasn't taking bribes. Jimmy would never do that, and I'm going to prove it."

He nodded. Fine with him. "I'll drive you to Jackson for that rental car."

"No." She finally turned back and looked him in the eye. "You have to go with me. Jason, too. I'm sorry."

Seemed like they were all sorry. But he had one up on her. He was good and confused, as well. "Did the authorities find the car in the ravine?"

"Yes."

"And the men who were shooting at us? Are they dead?"

"Yes."

"Then it seems my role in this should be over."

"There were only two bodies in the car."

A heaviness bore down on his chest. "You know that for sure?"

"That's how many they recovered. Two." She held

up her fingers, in case he needed to count. "I need you to come back with me."

Not, "Seth Wallace wants" or, "the system needs" or even his presence was required for justice's sake. She needed him.

The fact that her personal plea felt different made him more than a little uncomfortable. "I suppose you'll get a promotion out of the deal?"

She frowned at him as if he didn't understand a thing. "The charges against Jimmy aren't true. I have to prove it. And the only way Seth will agree to give me a look at the case against Jimmy is to bring you back to Denver."

Loyalty, not ambition.

He shook his head. No matter how good her reason, his hadn't changed. And his resolve hadn't weakened, not one bit. "I'll take you to Jackson. If that isn't enough for you, you can walk."

"Stop." The little voice ripped through the tension between them.

They both turned toward Jason. Tears pooled in blue eyes and streaked round cheeks. "No fighting."

His small voice hit Nick with the wallop of a thousand-pound kick to the gut. Jason had been so young when he and Gayle had last been together. He couldn't remember all the arguing, could he? Or had he been exposed to arguing since? Not that it mattered. Although his argument with Melissa was different than the ones he'd had with Gayle over…everything…he was replaying the discord just as he was replaying the attraction. Wasn't he? Or did it just make things easier to think so?

He focused on Jason, trying to push his questions to

the back of his mind. His son was the most important person in the world. He needed to focus on making him feel comfortable and safe and at home on the ranch. Arguing with Melissa certainly wasn't going to accomplish that, and neither was obsessing over the similarities and differences between her and Gayle.

He reached out a hand and awkwardly patted his son on the shoulder. "I'm sorry, Buddy. We won't fight anymore."

Melissa gathered Jason into her arms. "No more fighting. We promise."

Jason burrowed his face into her shoulder, his free hand finding her hair and tangling it in his fingers.

She glanced up at Nick.

Nick gave her a nod, careful not to meet her eyes. He hoped she realized agreeing to stop arguing didn't mean he'd given in. Jason was safe at the Circle J, and that wasn't something Nick would risk. Not for anyone.

Out of the corner of his eye, he saw Melissa tilt her wrist, giving her watch a glance. "Looks like it's about that time," she said.

Nick glanced at the wall clock. He hadn't realized it was getting so late. "Okay, Buddy. Why don't we head in to bed?"

Jason frowned and shook his head. "Don't want to."

"I'll read you a story." He fished a book from one of the boxes and held it up. "How about this one?"

The little guy shook his head and went back to playing with cars.

Nick could feel Melissa watching him. So now what did he do? No kid liked to go to bed, right?

"Maybe you should take a little of your own horse-back riding advice."

He glanced up at Melissa. "What's that?"

"Take control. Focus on what you want to have happen."

He brought his attention back to his son. Served him right to have his words thrown back at him. Still, she might have a point. He supposed he should just pick the little guy up and go.

He stepped through the jumble of boxes and zeroed in on Jason. Bending down, he held out his hands to scoop the little boy up.

Something inside made him hesitate.

"No."

Nick wasn't sure when he'd ever heard such a piercing scream. He slipped his hands under Jason's armpits.

"No, no, no." Jason thrashed, screaming as if he was sure Nick was going to kill him. "I don't got to. You're not my mommy! You're not my mommy! I hate you! I want to go home!"

Nick knew little kids had tantrums, especially ones who had been through as much emotional upheaval as Jason in the past few days. The child psychologist at the hospital had warned him about just this thing. He knew he should hold his ground. Be firm and patient, just like he'd be with a stubborn horse. But somehow his son's screams stunned the will right out of him.

He released the squirming little body and glanced at Melissa. "You want to try?"

She smiled at Jason. "Choose some toys to sleep with you, Buddy." She stood and grasped his hand.

Like flipping a switch, the little guy's screaming

stopped. Hand in hand with Melissa, he scurried around the den, gathering cars and action figures. Finally he and Nick exchanged stiff good-nights, and Jason followed Melissa into his bedroom.

Nick watched them go, his arms hanging useless by his sides. It was stupid to feel rejected by a four-year-old who didn't want to go to bed. He knew that. But that's how he felt all the same. It was as if everything Gayle said had been right all along.

He shook his head. When he'd thought about bringing his son home, he'd had visions of tucking him in bed and watching over him while he slept, knowing he was safe. The thing he'd yearned for most these past three years.

Things weren't working out remotely as he'd planned.

He lifted his hat from his head and ran his fingers through his hair before replacing it. He could sit here and feel sorry for himself all night, but what would that get him? It wouldn't convince Melissa and her boss that they didn't need him to go back to Denver. It wouldn't find out where the other two drive-by shooters disappeared to. And it wouldn't make Jason fall in love with the ranch and his father.

First things first.

He lowered himself to the couch and picked up Gayle's papers and started putting them back in the box. Melissa could take the box with her, but he and Jason were staying put. He just had to convince her of that.

By the time Melissa came back, he had his strategy laid out. At least he hoped so.

Melissa beat him to the punch. "Can I talk to you? I want to explain."

"Sure."

She walked into the room and lowered herself down to a sturdy chair next to the couch. "I wanted to tell you everything I learned. I don't want you to think I'm hiding anything from you."

"I appreciate that, but it's not going to change my mind."

She held up a hand, a plea to stop and hear her out.

He supposed he owed her that much. And he had to admit, he'd like some answers. "Go ahead."

She filled him in. When she got to the part about a gang members being the ones trying to kill him, he raised his hand for her to stop. "So if they are so dangerous, how does going back to Denver help?"

"You can identify the men in the car. Help us figure out who we're looking for. And I can protect you."

"You're protecting me right here."

"I need to take the boxes back. I need to make sure Sanchez is put away for life for what he did to Gayle. I need to find out about the rest of Calhoun's investigation and clear Jimmy's name." She paused, as if giving him a chance to join her commitment.

He had to give her credit. She'd told him exactly what she intended to do. It was time for him to do the same. "Listen, Melissa, as much as I appreciate you trying to keep me informed, and as sorry I am about your mentor, I have to do what's right for Jason. He's more important than anything that is playing out in Denver."

A dog barked out near the barn.

Nick cocked his head. He hoped it wasn't a grizzly

nosing around for garbage or horse feed to fatten up on before fast approaching hibernation. "And what's right for Jason is to stay here at the ranch."

The dog's barking grew more alarmed.

A bad feeling pricked the back of Nick's neck.

Melissa moved to the edge of the couch. "Is something wrong out there?"

Nick reached under the lamp's shade and switched off the light. "Better check." He crossed to the front window. Stepping to the side of the frame, he split the blinds with his fingers and peered outside.

At first all he saw was darkness, save the glow of a nearly full moon. The barn hulked in the distance, locked up tight, the yard light shining over a vacant yard. He could see the big trash Dumpster, safely surrounded by tall grizzly fence. Horses stirred in the corral, none showing the fear a grizzly or black bear would inspire. "It looks like the dog is just—"

Something stirred closer to the house, on the other side of his pickup. He narrowed his eyes, trying to make out the difference between movement and shadow.

"What is it?" Melissa whispered from just behind his shoulder.

Slowly Nick's eyes adjusted to the dim light. He could make out the silhouette of a man crouching behind the truck. Something shifted in the sagebrush beyond the corner of the house. Another man. And this one…this one held…

His throat went dry. "Melissa, go get Jason. Do it now."

"Nick?" Melissa flinched at the tremble in her voice. She was a trained officer. She knew how to control her emotions, do what needed to be done. She didn't feel rattled and weak. She took charge.

So why had the alarm in his voice sent a tremor through her she couldn't control?

"Get Jason. Go."

"What's going on?" She brought her hand to her hip. Her fingers brushed her holster and the rough grip of her gun.

"There are men out front. At least two. One is carrying an assault rifle."

Assault rifle? Melissa's heart stuttered in her chest. "We need to call 911." She snapped open her holster and drew her pistol. Not that a handgun would be much good against an assault rifle.

She pounded back the thought and started for the door leading to the common areas of the house and the guest rooms.

Nick grabbed her arm. "I'll call. Get Jason. He… he'll handle this better with you."

She closed her mouth without saying a word and started across the den. She could hear the thunk of Nick's strides behind her, veering off to the master bedroom. Melissa slipped into Jason's room. Moonlight glowed from the window above his bed.

She knelt down and eyed the tiny lump under the covers. "Jason? Buddy? Time to wake up." She peeled back the comforter to reveal the little guy, fingers twirling in his hair, thumb securely in his mouth. A tightening sensation gripped the base of her throat.

Swallowing hard, she slipped her hands underneath the sleeping boy and gathered him toward her. He reached for her neck, and she held him tight against her chest. A thick blanket lay on the bed. She grabbed it and wrapped it around him. Pushing to her feet, she scurried from the room.

Nick met her at the door, a rifle in one hand. He glanced at Jason, then back to Melissa. "There only seems to be the two of them."

At least that was good news, even if they were still outgunned. "You call the sheriff?"

"He's on his way, but there isn't a chance he'll get here in time to be much help. I don't want the two of you around when they decide to make their move."

He wanted them to leave the house? "It seems like it would be safer in here than outside."

He gave his head an abrupt shake. "Not once the fire starts."

"Fire?"

"I've been watching them. One is toting around a gas can. One guess as to what he intends to use it for."

That changed a lot of things. She shifted her grip on Jason, getting ready to hand him off to Nick.

He gave his head a shake. "No. You take him out the back. Make for the barn."

"When they start the fire, they'll be looking for us to run." And no doubt they'll be looking to take them out with the assault rifle when they did.

"That's why you're going to be gone before the fire starts."

"Me?" She couldn't have heard him right.

"You and Jason." He held up the hunting rifle. "I'll keep them distracted until you get away."

"It's my job to protect you. You'll take Jason. I'll stay."

He shook his head, as if he couldn't even consider such a thing. "I know how to shoot. Spent most of my life with a rifle in hand."

"There's no place for chivalry here. I'm not some weak female. This is my job. And you're all Jason has."

He paused for a moment, then turned away from her. "I'll grab you a coat. It's cold out there."

"Didn't you hear anything I said?"

"Jason has a stronger bond with you." He strode across the room and pulled open a closet door. Grabbing a shearling coat off one of the hangers, he carried it back to her. "I know the lay of the ranch in the dark. You don't. Even if you can hold them off and get out before they manage to burn down the house, you aren't going to know where to go. Are you?"

She hated not having an answer.

"That's why you're taking Jason and getting out of here now. Before things get crazy."

She pulled in a shaky breath. She didn't like having to rely on anyone to take care of her, certainly not cowboy Nick Raymond. But he had a practical point. And if they were going to make this work, she couldn't waste time arguing about it. Jason's life depended on what they did next.

She took the coat from Nick's hand. Adjusting Jason from side to side, she slipped into the sleeves and pulled it tight around her. "I go to the barn. Then what?"

"Throw a saddle on Bernie."

Bernie? It took her a second to connect the name with the horse Jason had been riding this afternoon. She shook her head. She'd had her first lesson in saddling a horse just a few hours ago, and now he wanted her to do it while he was having a shootout with men carrying assault rifles?

He looked her straight in the eye. "You can do it."

The way he said it, she almost believed she could. "Once I have the horse saddled, then what? Wait for you?"

"Don't wait. Ride straight past the pen where we were this afternoon. Follow the path. There's a cabin a few miles out, near the waterfall. We use it for overnight trips into the mountains. I'll meet you there."

And if you don't show? Melissa didn't say it, but the thought ran through her mind all the same. At least if they'd stayed in Denver, she could call for backup. Out here, they were on their own.

She and Jason would be on their own.

"Wait till I get off a round to make your move." Nick leaned forward as if taking one last look at the son he'd searched for all these years. Straightening, he thrust the shotgun into her hand, spun on his heel and bounded up the steps with his rifle.

Melissa watched him go, maybe for the last time.

Holding the boy against her shoulder and her weapon in one hand, she slipped out the back door to wait for the first crack of gunfire.

Chapter Eight

Nick crept across the hardwood floor of one of the second-floor guest rooms. Reaching the window, he slid up the sash, staying low so he couldn't be seen from below. He'd tried to convince Melissa he had this plan in hand, but in reality, he was far from sure it would work.

He squinted into the darkness. The men he'd seen from downstairs had moved closer to the house. From this vantage point, he could see that one had an assault rifle slung over his shoulder and both carried gas cans. They sidled along the front, closing in on the porch. Even now, he couldn't get a clear shot. Once they were under the porch overhang, he wouldn't be able to see them at all.

Time to make his move. He just hoped he could keep them busy enough so they didn't have time to round the house and intercept Melissa and Jason.

He slipped the barrel of his rifle through the open space between window frame and sash. He looked through the sight and picked out a spot as close to the men as he could get. At this angle, a hit would be miraculous. But at least he could send them scurrying for cover.

Taking a deep breath, he squeezed the trigger.

The crack echoed off the mountains. The men below swore and ducked for cover.

Nick fired another round then pulled the rifle barrel back just inside the outer window frame. He couldn't see any sign of the men. He held his breath, listening for a hint of movement from below.

He just hoped to hell Melissa had made her run for it. As long as she reached the horse and got Jason and herself to safety, this would all work out. He let out the breath he'd been holding and pulled in another. His pulse thunked in his ears, seeming almost as loud as the shots had been. A porch light flicked off, then another. Darkness cloaked the yard. Nick stared into the black night, willing his eyes to adjust to the glow from stars and moon.

A shot exploded from below. The upper sash shattered. Glass rained down.

He jolted back from the window. Shards of glass covered his shirt. He brushed his fingers through his hair and across his face. They came back sticky with blood.

Damn. He couldn't feel any pain. Adrenaline had likely numbed it. He had no idea how badly he'd been cut. But it didn't matter. He needed to keep the pressure on the men. He couldn't let them have the chance to circle the house. Not until he was sure Melissa and Jason were safely away.

He wiped his hand on his jeans and brought the rifle to his shoulder. If he rose high enough to see below the window, he would be visible to the man with the assault rifle. He would likely be dead before he could squeeze off a round. He would have to fire blind and hope the sound itself would force them to stay behind cover.

He fingered the trigger and pulled. The crack rang through the room and echoed through the darkness outside. He squeezed again. And again.

An answering shot crashed through the room. Wood splintered from the window frame. Nick dove to the floor.

Gunshots roared from outside, one after another. Wood, drywall and glass rained over him. Dust filled his throat, choking him.

The shots stopped. Nick gathered his rifle. If it was him down there, he'd have the window lined up in his sights, waiting for the first sign of movement to squeeze the trigger. It was too risky to take another shot from this window. He had to get out of here, find another position.

The scent of gasoline mixed with the scent of gunpowder and construction dust.

Oh hell. He needed to find another shot, and he needed to do it now.

Keeping low, he crept from the room, glass crunching under his boots. He made it to the hallway before another round came crashing through the window. He broke into a run and raced past three doors. When he reached the fourth guestroom, he slipped inside and moved to the window.

Nick inched up the window's lower sash and leaned close to the opening. Nothing but the low murmur and sporadic whinnies of horses moving nervously in the corral broke the night's still. Nick raised his head slowly above the bottom of the window frame and peered into the darkness.

His eyes searched for something to latch on to, a spark of flame, a shadow, a rustle of movement. Seconds passed. All he could see was endlessly swimming blackness. He strained to hear voices, movement or breathing from the men below.

A sound reached him. Faint and growing fainter. But Nick knew what it was. Footsteps. Running away. He was sure of it. But it wasn't a retreat. Far from it. They were circling the side of the house...and heading straight for the barn.

MELISSA FOLDED THE WESTERN saddle's fender up to the seat and slipped the stirrup over the horn to hold it. Taking a deep breath, she heaved the monstrosity up to her chest and took a run at poor Bernie.

The gelding didn't flinch. The saddle landed on the pad she'd balanced on his back. She grabbed on to it, trying to keep it from slipping over the other side.

So far, so good.

Adjusting pad and saddle so they were straight, she released what Nick had called the *off* stirrup and raised the *near* one. Now to strap the thing on. Hands shaking, she fitted the latigo strap through the big ring buckle on the end of the girth. She yanked the strap up, bringing the girth snug against the horse's belly. Then gritting her teeth, she pulled it as tight as she could and secured the metal prong in the leather strap's hole.

Another loud crack echoed through the night.

Her hands jerked, as they had with every gunshot. Jason let out a whimper.

She blotted her worries for Nick from her mind and craned her neck to see the boy. He was curled up on a rectangular bag of pine shavings. Thumb and fingers in their customary positions, he looked as if he wanted more than anything to crawl into a stall and hide.

Precisely what she wanted, too.

She plastered what she hoped was a reassuring smile to her lips. "It's okay, Buddy. We won't have to listen to that much longer. We're going to ride right out of here. Won't that be fun?"

He nodded, but he didn't look like he thought any of this was remotely fun. She had to admit, neither did she.

She brought her attention back to the horse. A bridle. That's what she needed next. She left the animal snapped in cross ties and darted back into the tack room. Hooks lined one wall, every one holding a bridle. For a second, she just stared at them. She'd recognized the saddle Nick had thrown on Bernie's back this afternoon, but she didn't have a clue which bridle he'd used. She remembered Nick adjusting the straps so the bit would hit the horse's mouth in the right place. If she didn't pick one that fit the horse, how in the world was she going to adjust the straps so it did?

She gasped in a breath and grabbed one that didn't have a metal bit at all, just a rawhide loop that looked like it fit around the horse's nose and a prickly rope that stood in for reins.

She returned to the horse and slipped it on his head. The contraption didn't look that different from the leather halter he had been wearing. She hoped it worked.

"Let's go, Jason," she said in the lightest voice she could manage. After checking the saddle to make sure the girth was still tight, she picked the little boy up and hoisted him onto the seat. Grabbing the rope, she led the gelding outside. Now to get on herself.

She looped the rope over the horse's head. Facing the horse's tail, she twisted the stirrup around and placed her boot inside like Nick had shown her.

The crunch of footsteps on gravel came from the direction of the house.

Her whole body seemed to leap on its own. Nick?

Gunfire exploded from the house.

Not Nick. Nick was still in the house. The footsteps weren't his.

The figure of a man rounded the corner of the barn. Shorter and slighter than Nick, he wore a black jacket and baggy jeans. In his hand he held a semiautomatic pistol.

Still balancing on one foot, Melissa reached for her gun. As she brought it up, gunfire spat again from the direction of the house.

Gravel and dirt sprayed into the air right in front of the gunman's feet.

He shimmied back, half running, half throwing his body back toward the barn corner.

Melissa searched the area where the gunfire had to have come. She could only see his silhouette, but she'd know those broad shoulders and cowboy hat anywhere. "Nick!"

"Go, go, go!" he yelled. He raised the rifle to his shoulder again and fired.

She vaulted herself onto Bernie's back. She missed

the saddle's seat, landing on the edge of the cantle and slipping to the flat skirt behind. It took a second for her to settle behind Jason. Holding the rope in one hand, she looped her other arm around the four-year-old and grabbed the saddle horn. Taking a deep breath, she brought her legs hard against the horse's side. Go forward. Go forward.

Bernie leaped forward into a bouncy trot.

The gait jarred up Melissa's spine. Her seat slipped with each jolt, her body listing to the side. She squeezed harder with her legs, half kicking this time.

The horse's gait broke into a smooth, rocking lope.

Regaining her balance, she squinted into the night. The corral fence streamed alongside them. Up ahead, the shadow of a mountain formed a dark outline surrounded by stars. The gelding's hooves beat rhythmically over packed dirt. It seemed like the right way. It had to be the right way.

Another crack of a gun sounded from behind.

She stifled the gasp before it escaped her mouth and concentrated on the way ahead. Nick had to be all right. He had to catch up with them at the cabin.

The horse carried them farther and farther from the ranch, leaving Nick behind. All alone against two armed men.

NICK LET OUT A RELIEVED breath. They'd made it. They'd gotten away. For a moment there, he thought he'd lost them both, Jason and Melissa.

The crack of a gunshot wiped the jumble of thoughts from his mind. He threw himself to the ground. The assault rifle. No doubt the one with the assault rifle had heard shooting near the barn and figured out he'd left the house. Now he had two gunmen to contend with and no real cover.

His breath rasped his throat. Sagebrush surrounded him, its strong smell permeating every inhale. The sage would make it hard to spot him in the dark, but he needed to find something solid. Something that would allow him to get off a few rounds without immediately giving away his location.

The guest cabins weren't far. If he could make it there, he could move from cabin to cabin, impossible to pin down.

Rifle out in front of him, he pulled his body forward with his elbows and pushed with his knees. His hand hit a prickly pear. He forced himself to ignore the stabs of the needle-like spines and keep moving.

His dog barked from inside the barn. A siren screamed in the distance.

Soon. One way or another, this would be over soon.

EVEN THOUGH THE TRIP had taken longer than Melissa could imagine, the cabin was right where Nick had said it would be. It was more than one cabin, actually. Three buildings clustered at the base of the mountain. The creek trickled nearby, as he'd described. And the constant roar of the nearby waterfall filled the air like the static of an untuned radio.

She was sure the setting was beautiful in the daylight. In darkness, after having just escaped armed men, not so much.

She'd slowed the horse to a jog, then to a walk. The

scent of hot horse stuck to her skin. Her hands ached from the death grip she'd had on rope and saddle horn. Her seat bones were so tender from bouncing on the saddle, they felt like they'd worn right through her flesh.

She glanced over her shoulder. Dark hulks flanked each side of the trail. She knew they were only sagebrush, but in the dark even the native plant life felt malevolent.

She suppressed a shiver. Releasing the saddle horn, she brought her arm around Jason's little body and gave him a hug. "We made it. Your daddy will be here soon."

He twisted around and looked up at her with big blue eyes. "I don't want to ride Bernie anymore."

Poor guy. He was likely as sore as she was. "I'm sure Bernie could use a break, too."

She piloted the horse up to the first cabin before bringing him to a halt. She dismounted first, swinging her right leg over and lowering herself to the ground with her left. Pain ached through her inner thighs. Her legs felt bowed like some cartoon cowboy, her knees too wobbly to hold her weight. She stood for a moment, clinging to Bernie's saddle to keep herself upright.

"I want to get down," Jason said, his voice holding a touch of whine.

Melissa willed her legs to function. She reached up, placing a hand on either side of the little boy's rib cage. "Okay. Here we go." She pulled him off the horse's back and lowered him to the ground.

Unlike her, Jason was able to walk as soon as his feet hit the earth. He shuffled across the beaten dirt path in his footed pajamas, the blanket she'd taken from his bed wrapped around him like a cloak.

Melissa took the rope and led the horse on one side and Jason on the other. She trudged past the cabin and to what appeared to be the barn. Letting them all inside, she reversed the process of saddling, stripping Bernie of saddle and pad. His back was wet with sweat. She hoped leaving him inside the barn would prevent him from getting a chill, but what did she know about taking care of a horse?

She just hoped Nick arrived soon. She was totally out of her element here…and more than a little worried.

Pushing the image of him holding his rifle at the ready—yelling at her to go—to the back of her mind, she dug the key he had given her from her pocket and let Jason and herself into the cabin.

The place was nicer than Melissa's apartment. Although it was much smaller than the ranch's main lodge, the setup was similar. A common room dominated the middle of the cabin, complete with a wood-burning stove. A kitchenette lined the opposite wall. And two bedrooms flanked one wall, in addition to the bathroom. Add the hardwood floors, and the timbers in the ceiling, it had precisely the right amount of rustic touch to appeal to rich city dwellers who wanted to feel like they were roughing it without actually doing so.

She led Jason to a big leather couch with a wooden frame. "Are you hungry? I might be able to find something in here to eat."

He shook his head. His thumb once again found his mouth.

She couldn't blame him. Hungry was the last thing

she was. She felt like she was on the edge of a cliff, waiting for a stiff wind to blow her off at any moment.

She eyed the wood stove, then looked back to Jason. A warm fire would feel nice. Safe. The problem was, she didn't know if they actually were safe. And if they weren't, a fire would only serve to tell whoever might be out there where they were.

She sat on the couch next to Jason and folded him in her arms, wrapping one side of the coat Nick had given her and the blanket from Jason's bed around both of them. She rested her hand on her hip, her fingers on the grip of her gun.

The minutes slowly ticked. Jason's eyelids drooped then closed. His warm little body rose and fell with deep, even breaths.

Outside, the wind picked up, its howl joining with the endless hiss of the falls. The air grew colder, and once again Melissa eyed the wood stove, then discarded the idea. How long would it take Nick to reach them? What if he never came? What if he was shot and dying all alone? What if she and Jason were next?

She hated not knowing. Hated this helpless, rudderless feeling. Hated waiting.

She was used to taking charge of situations, and she liked that. Not having to rely on anyone. Not being let down. This made her feel like she was as much of a child as Jason. A child with no one to care for her and nowhere to turn.

The door knob rattled.

Melissa jolted upright. Nick? Or had one of the men followed from the ranch?

She pulled her Glock from its holster. She shifted

Jason to one side. Slowly, she slipped her arm free and moved off the couch. She crept to the kitchen, between the door and the boy, and took cover behind an angle of kitchen cupboard.

The weapon felt sure in her hands. She took a calm breath despite her hammering pulse.

The lock rattled once more. The knob turned. The door creaked open.

Nick stepped inside.

He wore only the shirt he'd been wearing earlier, no coat.

A cut lanced one cheek, dried blood staining his face and neck. Dust and debris clung to his hat and sparkled in his hair.

A breath shuddered from Melissa's lungs. She slid her finger out of the trigger guard. She lowered the barrel to point at the floor.

He shut and locked the door and crossed the few feet to her side. His eyes darted to Jason and back to her. "You're both okay?"

A sob of relief balled in her chest. A sob she couldn't let free.

Her knees felt weak, as if they could no longer hold her. What was wrong with her? She'd been cool, even calm with the gun in her hand, but as soon as she caught a glimpse of Nick's face the rest had caught up. The worry, the fear…she stepped toward him.

He wrapped his arms around her and pulled her to his chest. "It's okay. It's all okay."

She knew what he was saying must be true. He was here, wasn't he? He obviously wasn't shot dead outside the corral. He was fine. But her brain somehow couldn't absorb the realization. She felt as if she was staring at a ghost, someone lost that she'd never see again.

She tilted her head back and stretched her arms around his neck. It was idiotic. Stupid to feel this way, but she didn't care. She had to feel he was alive, that he was really there.

She had to feel she was, too.

She didn't move to kiss him. She didn't have to. He brought his lips down on hers, strong and warm and alive. Something opened inside her. Something strong and invincible but more vulnerable than any feeling she'd ever known.

Chapter Nine

Nick had no business kissing Melissa Anderson, but he was still disappointed when she pushed him away.

"I can't...we can't...." She spread her hands over her chest as if shielding her heart from him.

"I know. I know. It was stupid. I'm sorry." He held up his hands, even though the only thing he wanted was to run them down her back, over her hips and pull her snug against him.

When the shooter had cornered her and Jason outside the barn, he'd feared he'd lost them both, never mind that she was never his to lose. And at this moment, all he wanted was to hold on to her for as long as he could.

"I was just...I don't know...worried. I wasn't sure you'd make it, and..."

"No need to explain. It won't happen again." He blew a breath through tight lips and forced himself to step away. Before the shooters had attacked, he'd told himself Melissa was just like Gayle. That alone had been more than enough reason for him to keep his attraction to her under wraps. But convenient as the lie was, he couldn't believe it any longer.

Gayle had been ambitious, always striving for more because that was what made her feel important. Melissa might be ambitious, too. But he had a feeling that was only a tiny sliver of the force that drove her. She talked about justice, about being there for her dead mentor with bone-deep passion. The way he felt about the ranch. The way he felt about his son.

But none of that changed the facts. None of it meant she would chuck her city life, her career, her friends and move to Middle-of-Nowhere, Wyoming. None of it meant she could ever be happy with him.

He turned away from her and paced across the room, his boots sounding on the hardwood floor.

He could hear Melissa draw a shaky breath behind him. "What happened? At the ranch? How did you get away?"

He turned back to face her. He'd much rather describe what had happened than dwell on impossible scenarios, impossible feelings. "The sheriff's department. As soon as the two heard sirens, they took off."

"So they weren't caught." She pursed her lips.

He could guess her thoughts. The men who killed Detective Bernard were still out there. Justice was yet to be served. But that wasn't what was going through his mind. Her goals hadn't changed. His had hit a brick wall.

He could waste time telling himself nothing had changed in the past few hours, but he'd be lying. Everything had changed. As soon as those men had set foot on his land with their assault rifles and gas cans, all his illusions of security had evaporated. Nothing was the same. And as a result, he needed to change, too. "I can't bring Jason back to the ranch. He's not safe there, and he won't be until these guys are stopped."

"So what are you going to do?"

He let a grin curl one side of his mouth. "I appreciate your restraint."

"Restraint?"

"I know you're chomping at the bit to bring up the DA's protective custody."

"Well?"

"You said the shooters in the car knew where Detective Bernard would be, that they waited for him."

She nodded.

"What's to say they won't know where we are? That whoever told them where to find the detective won't tell them where to find us?"

"We can keep the information restricted. Only Seth and I need to know."

"How about only you?"

"You have a problem with Seth?"

"No."

She narrowed her eyes.

"Okay, I'd like to use his power tie to wipe that smug smile off his face. And the whole threatening to throw me in jail thing might have rubbed me the wrong way, but other than that…"

A chuckle sounded low in her throat. "Okay. Only me. But I have to ask. Why the change of heart?"

"I tried it my way. I guess it's time to try yours."

"That easy, huh?"

"Not easy. But after tonight, it's clear. Until you catch those two and whomever else is behind this mess, we can't have our lives back. And if I help, maybe we can solve this a little faster."

She watched him for a long while. Finally she walked toward him.

For a long second, he thought she might let him take her back in his arms, let him claim her lips once again. And as disastrous as he knew getting involved with another woman who would never stick around would be, for that second, he let himself imagine.

She pulled up short. "We'll ride back to the ranch tomorrow? Head out from there?"

He nodded. "I have to make arrangements. My foreman can supervise repairs to the ranch house and grounds."

Her gaze flicked first to one bedroom door, then the other.

Silence hummed through the room. She stood only ten feet from him. One step, maybe two, and she'd be close enough to touch. "One has a king bed, the other two fulls. Your choice."

She curled her lower lip inward and trapped it between her teeth. "I'll take the king. That way Jason can sleep with me. I wouldn't want him to wake up alone."

He dropped his gaze to the floor. "Yes. Good thinking."

DENVER HADN'T CHANGED much in the two days Melissa had been gone, but it felt different all the same. Safer. More secure. Like a favorite blanket she could wrap around her shoulders and shield herself from the unknown.

She glanced at Nick dozing in the passenger's seat next to her, his Stetson tipped low over his eyes. In the back, Jason watched a video where animated creatures danced and sang. The catchy tunes rolled over and over. She'd found on the long drive down that if she concentrated on them hard enough, she could chase thoughts of last night's kiss from her mind. At least for a second or two.

At the moment, she was having less luck on that front.

It would take more than ear worms to permanently wipe away the memory of Nick's lips on hers. The way something inside her had opened up when he touched her. The weak feeling that had flooded her limbs and centered in her core.

She couldn't let it happen again.

She'd been thrown off balance in Wyoming. The mountains, the horses, the whole cowboy fantasy. And that night, the way Nick had given Jason and her a chance to escape, the fear of being alone in the wilderness, the relief when he'd stepped through that door... all of it had sapped her will. It had reduced her to a quivering mass of need.

She focused on the concrete strength of buildings, the vibrancy of the interstate, the mountains only distant shadows. Now she was back in her world, in her city, things would be different. Here she was strong. Independent. Here she didn't need a swaggering cowboy to teach her how to ride or rescue her from gunmen.

Here she didn't need to rely on anyone but herself.

"So where are we headed?" Nick tilted his hat back and looked at her through one eye.

Melissa carefully focused on the interstate and the thick traffic flowing on either side of the pickup. "Seth will expect me to report first thing."

"What are you going to tell him?"

"The truth. That you're back. That you're willing to help."

"And he's going to insist on taking us into protective custody."

"He can't do that if he doesn't know where you are."

She could feel his skepticism, and she couldn't blame him. She'd be skeptical of putting her fate in someone else's hands, too.

"I'm not going to tell Seth. And I've been watching the road behind us. No one is following."

"What if they're waiting for us in Denver?"

"First, I don't think they have any reason to think we've returned."

One corner of his mouth quirked up in a hint of a dry smile. "I'll have to give you that one. I'm still not sure it makes sense to me at times."

"There you go." She returned the half smile. "And we'll be careful. Take precautions."

"What's your plan?"

"Jimmy had a cabin, a place that was just his that he didn't let many other people know about. It's not as fancy as yours. It's kind of a dump, really. But it's somewhat close to the city, yet it's isolated, too. I thought I'd ask Tammy if we could stay there."

"Tammy?"

"Jimmy's wife." The back of her throat ached at the thought of what her friend must be going through since her husband had been shot down in the street. She felt horrible that she couldn't be there to help her deal with it all.

Of course, with all of Tammy's friends and nearly everyone on the force paying their respects, she wouldn't have been alone the past couple of days. But the two of them had a bond unlike anything Melissa shared with her own mother. She felt terrible that days had passed and she hadn't been able to give Tammy so much as a phone call. "Problem is, I'm not sure what Tammy knows or doesn't know about Cory Calhoun's investigation of Jimmy."

"You going to tell her? It might be better coming from someone she knows."

She wasn't so sure. "I'm not sure how she'll react."

"She'll find out eventually."

"I know. And she might take it better coming from me, but not until I have some facts that disprove Calhoun's conclusions."

"Seems to me if Tammy knew about the investigation, she might be able to help."

"You might be right, but…I can't explain it. I just don't want to make things harder on her than they already are. Not if I don't have to."

"Okay. My lips are sealed." He put his fingers to his lips as if to illustrate.

For a second, Melissa could again feel the pressure of his kiss, the weakness inside. She yanked her focus back to the road. Her cheeks felt hot, and she lowered the fan on the truck's heater.

How she was going to handle staying in Jimmy's cabin with Nick, she had no clue. At least Jason would be there, too. And Nick himself seemed wary today. After his experience with his ex-wife, she doubted he was looking for any kind of entanglement.

At least she could hope.

She exited the interstate and piloted the truck through familiar streets. She circled the block three times. Satisfied no one was staking out the place, she turned onto a quiet street and pulled the truck to the curb down the block from the modest adobe house she'd always thought of as a second home. "This is it."

She and Nick climbed out of the truck, and Nick collected Jason from the backseat. As the three of them walked up the sidewalk to the front door, Melissa couldn't help but notice how much like a little family they probably appeared to neighbors peeking through their blinds. She'd never planned on a family. Never wanted one. She'd seen too much of what her mother went through to ever put herself in such a vulnerable position.

Tossing her hair out of her eyes, she stabbed the doorbell with a finger.

The door swung inward and Tammy appeared in the doorway. A thin woman, Tammy had always reminded Melissa of a doll she had as a kid made of wire with a rubber coating, strong and flexible. But now her bones appeared as fragile as that wire had gotten over time, and her skin draped loosely over that brittle frame. New lines etched her younger-than-her-years complexion. And blue eyes that used to sparkle at Jimmy B's jokes looked puffy and rimmed in pink.

Those eyes flared wide. Tammy lurched out onto the step and wrapped her arms around Melissa. She clung as if her life depended on it. "I called your office. They said you were on vacation."

Melissa jerked back to stare at her. "Vacation?"

Tammy gathered her tight once more, as if worried she would slip away. "It didn't make sense to me. I mean, Jimmy dies and you go on vacation? I didn't know what to think."

"I wasn't on vacation, Tammy. I'm sorry I couldn't get here sooner."

Tammy held on for a few more seconds, then released her and pulled back a few inches to study Melissa's face. "What happened to you? Something bad."

Great. She must look as tired as she felt. "I'm fine."

Tammy looked past Melissa's shoulder at Nick and Jason. "And you brought someone?" She looked back to Melissa, unspoken questions written all over her expression.

Melissa stepped to the side and made introductions. "Jason was the boy Jimmy was collecting from the hotel. Nick was there, too."

"A witness? They didn't tell me there was a witness." Her lips pursed. "They hardly told me anything."

Melissa let out a breath. So Tammy didn't know Jimmy was under investigation? She hoped not. If anything good could be said about the silence surrounding this case, it was that she might be able to diffuse it before Tammy ever had to know. "There's more. Can we come in?"

"Of course."

Tammy led them into the well-worn living room Melissa had come to think of as home. The smell of Jimmy's stale cigars hung in the air like a fading memory. They sat on the wood-frame couch where Melissa had watched John Elway win two Super Bowls, Jimmy shouting his usual colorful profanities at the refs for every flag against the Broncos. In the corner, Jimmy's leather recliner sat empty. Melissa's throat started to ache.

"Can I get you something? A beer? Coffee? Juice? Something to eat? I made cookies."

Jason's eyes brightened, and he gave a little hop. "Cookies? Can I have cookies?"

"Sure, Buddy," Nick said. He exchanged looks with Melissa, then looked back to Tammy. "Come to think of it, I'm a little hungry, too. I think some homemade cookies would really hit the spot."

"Chocolate chip." Tammy smiled at Melissa. "They always were your favorite."

"Not for me, thanks." Melissa did love Tammy's chocolate chip cookies, but at the moment she felt anything but hungry. Besides, with Nick and Jason busy chomping on cookies, it would give her a chance to talk with Tammy one-on-one, probably what Nick was trying to communicate with that glance. "Go ahead, you guys."

Melissa watched while Tammy set Jason and Nick up at the kitchen table with cookies, two big glasses of milk and Jason's toy cars. She'd forgotten Tammy's compulsion of serving during stressful times. It never failed, if you or she or anyone within a hundred-mile radius were going through a bad time, Tammy wanted to feed all humans in her vicinity. It felt so warm and familiar it made Melissa want to cry. "Has anyone from the force or the D.A.'s office been here?"

"Of course." She motioned to the kitchen. "My countertops are heaped with bars and brownies and my fridge is stuffed with casseroles."

And yet she made cookies? Classic Tammy. "I mean in an official capacity. Asking questions, that kind of thing?"

The lines on either side of Tammy's mouth deepened. "Yes."

"Who?"

"He said his name was Calhoun. From the D.A."

"I know him," Melissa said.

Tammy nodded. "I know they have to run an investigation every time an officer fires his weapon, but from what this Calhoun told me, Jimmy didn't even get that chance."

"What did he ask you about?"

"That didn't make a lot of sense, either."

"How so?"

"He wanted to know Jimmy's mental state and how healthy our finances were. He even asked about our marriage. I asked him what he was getting at, but he wouldn't tell me. It was weird."

Not so weird from where Melissa was standing. It sounded like Calhoun was digging for something he could use to justify the theory that Jimmy had suddenly fallen to corruption. "Did anyone from the force ask you questions?"

"No." Tammy narrowed her eyes, as if she was trying to figure out where Melissa was coming from. "Should they have asked me something?"

"No, no. I was just wondering."

Her expression didn't change. "Is there something going on between the D.A.'s office and the Denver P.D.?"

Melissa held up her hands, palms out. "I've been gone, so I don't know much more than you do. In fact, I probably know less. That's why I'm asking. Did you talk to anyone from the force?"

"Ben Marris was here."

"Marris? What did he say?"

"Besides wanting to know who I thought should be pallbearers?" Her eyes glistened. She blinked furiously, but tears escaped and trickled down her cheeks despite her efforts.

She rubbed her friend's shoulder. Tammy swayed beneath her touch. She felt as breakable as she looked. "I'm so sorry you have to go through this."

She sniffed and dabbed at her cheeks with a tissue. "I know you are, Melissa."

"I want you to know I'm here. Okay, Tammy? I'm here whenever you need me."

"Helping them catch the boys that did it and making sure they go to prison will be enough for me, Melissa. Jimmy always said you were the best at your job he'd seen for a long time. And after the situation you grew up in…" She blew her nose, then focused on Melissa, lashes spiked with tears. "He was sad when you went to the D.A.'s office, but he was so proud, too. Said they needed someone like you."

The room grew misty. Melissa willed her eyes to stay dry. She hoped she was as good at her job as Jimmy thought. Judging from the little bit Seth had told her, it would take every ounce of grit she had to set things right and nail the men behind this. Jimmy deserved that and far more. "Did Jimmy get any threats here at home? Any strange calls? Visitors?"

"I thought he was killed protecting..." She nodded toward Jason, eating his cookies in the kitchen. "Do you think they were out to kill Jimmy all along?"

"We don't know for sure, but it looks like Jimmy might have been the target."

Tammy reached back and gripped the leather lounge chair, as if she needed it for support.

Melissa gave her a long moment. "Anything you can think of could be helpful."

"There were threats here and there. But there are always threats here and there. He was a detective. He arrested bad people. Sometimes they made empty threats. It wasn't anything that seemed unusual."

"Do you know where the recent threats were coming from?"

"No. He kept most of it at work."

"What did you notice here at home?"

"Nothing, really." She perched on the lounge chair's arm, folded her hands and stuffed them between her knees. "Cory Calhoun asked that same question, though."

"About the threats?"

"Yes. I forgot about that. And something else."

"What?"

"He asked me if I had ever heard Jimmy talk about a woman named Gayle Rodgers."

Calhoun, making his case. Or jamming facts in to fit his theories, anyway. "What did you tell him?"

"That I'd heard him say the name.

"The night before…" She looked up to the ceiling and paused for a moment. When she resumed, her voice sounded rough and raw. "He was arguing with someone on the phone about her. That's all I remember. But it wasn't someone threatening him or anything. It was someone at work."

"Another cop?"

"I don't know. I could just tell it was someone in law enforcement by the words he used. Shop talk, you know. At least that's how it seemed to me."

"What was he arguing about?"

"He said he had a lead. He said he was planning to take it all the way if he had to." Shaking her head, she reached into her pocket, pulled out a tissue and dabbed her eyes. "I wouldn't even remember it except that he just had that tone in his voice, you know? That determined tone that he got sometimes. Whenever I heard it, I knew he was going to get his way."

Maybe someone else had recognized that tone, too. Maybe that's why someone had to stop him. "Did Calhoun ask for anything? Like your home phone records or Jimmy's cell…?"

"No."

Interesting. He must have gone through the phone company to get a record of current calls, but to do that, he'd either need a warrant from the court or Tammy's permission. Melissa would love to see those records herself. "Do you have your last few months of phone records?"

Tammy narrowed her eyes on Melissa. "Why are

you asking all these questions, Melissa? What is going on that you haven't told me?"

"Just tying up some loose ends."

"It's more than that. You're acting like Jimmy is the one being investigated." Tammy's mouth flattened to a hard line. Her eyebrows pulled low. "You and your district attorney, you're trying to prove Jimmy did something wrong. He's not even in the grave and you… How dare you?"

Chapter Ten

"Hold on." Nick couldn't sit back and watch this anymore. This might be Melissa's friend and Melissa's city, but he just wasn't built to let things fall apart in front of him and not at least try to stand up and take charge.

He pushed up from his chair. In two steps, he was in front of Tammy Bernard. "Melissa doesn't deserve this. She's trying to clear your husband's name, damn it. Calhoun is the one investigating."

Melissa's hand tightened on his shoulder. "Nick. No."

"There *is* an investigation then. Into Jimmy." Tammy's voice barely rose above a whisper.

The woman sounded shell-shocked, her voice monotone, and for a moment Nick could understand why Melissa had wanted to shield her from additional emotional stress. Too bad they didn't have the luxury to just sweep any unpleasantness under the rug and focus on cookies and milk. "Melissa just found out about it last night."

Melissa took Tammy's hands in hers and stared straight into the older woman's eyes. "I didn't want you to know. Not until I cleared it all up. You have too much to deal with as it is."

Tammy shook her head. "No…no. I need to know. What do they say Jimmy did?"

"Melissa?" Jason called from the kitchen.

Melissa glanced at Nick, the look holding a silent plea.

"Melissa," Tammy said. "Jimmy was always straight with me. He always trusted me enough to tell me the truth. You need to be straight with me, too."

Nick gave Melissa a nod. He was far from sure his son would be content with him as a substitute for Melissa, but he'd give it a try.

Melissa let out a heavy sigh and started explaining the suspicions of bribery and ties to drug gangs. With each word, her voice grew more rough and raw.

Nick circled back to the kitchen table where Jason was watching, his toy cars held in frozen hands. He had devoured his cookies and sucked down most of his milk. Nick slid back into his chair at the kitchen table and picked up a blue Camaro, the only tool left in the distraction arsenal. "Let's play cars."

Jason shook his head, craning his neck to see Melissa.

Nick remembered the horseback-riding advice Melissa had tossed back at him. *Take control. Focus on the result you want*. He zoomed the little car across the oak surface.

Jason's eyes flicked down to the car. His fingers tightened around the vehicle in his hand.

Nick made his car take a sharp turn, imitating the screech of tires on pavement. Taking a looping detour around cookie plate and milk glass, he drove it back toward him.

Jason moved his car, bringing it alongside Nick's. He blew air through his lips, providing engine sound effects for their game.

So far, so good. He made a fishtailing turn with the Camaro and started back the other way, an ear cocked for the conversation in the living room. Melissa might never forgive him for confirming Tammy's fears, but at least on the Jason front he might be on to something. He could hope.

BY THE TIME MELISSA explained everything she knew about Calhoun's investigation, she felt she'd been wrung dry. At least Tammy had dealt with it far better than Melissa had feared. The older woman had loaded her up with the past year or so of phone records, none of which showed any suspicious calls. And when they left, with cabin keys in hand, all three of them were weighted down with some form of casserole or desert.

But before they could go to the cabin, Melissa had to talk to Seth. As soon as she left Nick and Jason parked on the street outside a playland-equipped McDonald's just a few blocks from the D.A.'s office, she felt strangely alone. And strangely uncomfortable. She half ran all the way to the office.

Melissa might have been alone when she stepped into Seth's office, but Seth wasn't. Cory Calhoun leaned back in one of the chairs in front of Seth's desk, ankle propped on knee. His orange hair looked extra bright against the pale of his skin. He turned squinty eyes on her. "Glad you're back, Melissa."

She'd bet he was glad. "Hi, Cory." She looked past him and focused on Seth.

For a man who prided himself on his looks, Seth was dangerously close to disheveled. Dark circles cupped under bloodshot green eyes. His hair appeared as if he'd raked his fingers through it a bit too often. And his red tie was slightly askew. No doubt these past few days had been tough on him, as well. She could only hope his patience was still intact. At least his patience with her, if not Calhoun. "I need to talk to you, Seth."

He nodded. "Have a seat."

"Alone." She didn't let her gaze slide to Calhoun, but she could sense the smug look that had to be on his face about now.

"Listen, I have enough on my plate without having to act as some sort of referee between you two."

Calhoun held up his beefy hands. "You don't have to worry about me. I'm just doing my job."

"And I'm not?"

"Let's just say I know this mess is a little more personal for you."

Damn right it was personal. Melissa managed to bite her tongue before the words slipped out. All she needed was Calhoun to convince Seth she was some kind of hysterical female who couldn't separate her personal feelings from the job. "I just want to find the truth, Cory. Same as you."

"Glad to hear everyone's so agreeable." Seth motioned to the chair next to Cory. "Have a seat and we can get started."

So Seth had planned their meeting to include

Calhoun. So much for privately questioning the preconceived notions of her fellow investigator.

She stepped to the chair and lowered herself into it. Carefully crossing her legs only at the ankles, she suppressed the urge to fold her arms. Best to appear open, relaxed, like she had nothing vital invested. She gave Seth a controlled, businesslike smile. "You were going to fill me in?"

"There's not a lot that you don't already know. Jimmy was accepting payoffs from Sanchez in return for ignoring the drug activities of him and his gang."

"Do you have proof of that?"

"I have witnesses," Calhoun said.

"Witnesses who don't have a reason to lie?"

Calhoun didn't answer.

Score one for Jimmy. "Do you know how the Latin Devils supposedly contacted him?"

Seth's green gaze flicked up to Calhoun then dropped back to the report. "Phone? In person?"

"All of the above."

"Really?" Melissa said. She pulled out her envelope of phone records. "Then why don't these calls show up on the phone company's records?"

Calhoun held out his hand.

Melissa turned away. She leaned forward and placed the copies on Seth's blotter.

Seth slapped the phone records down on top of Calhoun's report and started perusing.

"There aren't any calls to Gayle Rodgers or gang members." She tossed a look Calhoun's way. "Jimmy was clean."

Calhoun snickered. "He could have communicated

some other way. Maybe they met in person. Maybe he used a cell phone we don't know about. There are a lot of explanations."

He was guessing. If he knew, that shouldn't be necessary. "I thought you had proof Jimmy was in touch with Sanchez."

"I have proof." He gestured to the report on Seth's desk. "Bernard and Sanchez had a history."

Again, it seemed Calhoun was assuming things he shouldn't assume. "Of course he *knew* Sanchez. Jimmy busted him twice. You don't have proof of any calls between them though, do you?"

"Not yet."

Seth looked up and met Melissa's eyes. "I'm sorry, Melissa. He's right. As encouraging as these records are, all they prove is that Jimmy wasn't sloppy."

Melissa shook her head. "Since when do you have to prove a man's innocence?"

Seth gave her a sympathetic tilt of the lips. "Since the press will be swarming all over this as soon as they get a whiff."

He had a point. The press loved police scandal, and it seemed as if they didn't require even a shred of evidence before splashing such rumors all over the front page and using them to lead their newscasts. But though she believed in Jimmy's innocence beyond a shadow of a doubt, she couldn't prove it. Not yet. But she might be able to open up different possibilities. "Have you ever considered that there might be something else going on here?"

Seth leaned forward, elbows on desk. "Something? Like what?"

"I don't know. But Jimmy had a brand-new lead about Gayle Rodgers's death. He was telling someone about it the night before he died."

"How do you know this?" Seth glanced down at the phone records, as if the answer might be right there in front of him.

"His wife remembers the call, but she's not certain of the time."

Calhoun arched his brows. "Who was he talking to?"

She glanced at Calhoun. "I don't know. *Yet.*"

"Well, I guess that's all the proof we could ask for." Calhoun brushed his palms together with a light clapping sound. "Case closed."

She felt like strangling the guy. "You're the one who has no evidence. This is a witch hunt."

Seth shook his head slowly, as if the movement took all his energy. "There are things you don't know about, Melissa."

"Then tell me. I thought that's why I was here."

Seth nodded to Calhoun.

Calhoun all but rubbed his hands together, eagerly this time. "We think Bernard was involved with Gayle Rodgers on the side."

The words hung in the air for several seconds before they sank in to Melissa's mind. Jimmy? And Nick's ex-wife? She shook her head. "Impossible."

"Not so impossible," Calhoun said, his voice strangely soft this time. "We have credit card charges for nearby hotel rooms. We have evidence that Gayle was buying little gifts a man might appreciate. And the landlord, he saw a boyfriend."

"That doesn't mean it was Jimmy."

"The landlord's description says different. Tall, good-looking, graying hair."

She still wouldn't believe it.

Calhoun went on. "We don't know why Gayle turned on him, woman scorned or something, but that's when she called our office."

"You have recordings of those calls? Specific information she offered?"

"We're getting it."

"What do you mean, you're getting it?"

"Just that. When I have more, I'm sure Seth will let you know." Calhoun focused a put-out look on Seth.

Seth nodded. "Go on. Tell her how the rest fits together."

"When Bernard found out Gayle Rodgers was in touch with us, he told Sanchez. Sanchez needs to protect his investment. Dirty cops aren't that easy to come by, you know. So he kills Gayle Rodgers, takes some stuff to make it look like a burglary gone bad."

Melissa had to admit, the scenario might be possible, but not for Jimmy. "Jimmy arrested Sanchez for Gayle's murder. Why would he do that if Sanchez killed to protect him?"

Calhoun shrugged a shoulder, as if none of these details mattered enough to bother him. "He didn't ask Sanchez to kill anybody. Just because he takes bribes doesn't mean he's a murderer. So he pops Sanchez for his crime. Figures it will make him right with the Lord or something, who knows?" Calhoun settled back in his chair like a man comfortable he had figured out all the answers.

She thought of the men in the sedan, men Nick saw, two of whom she'd caused to crash through the guardrail and into the ravine. "And the men who shot Jimmy?"

"Sanchez's gang brothers—fine, upstanding members of society that they are. They pull a drive-by to pay back the cop who framed their amigo."

"You know who the shooters are? You got an ID on them?"

Another shrug from Calhoun. "They were gang members. We're working on the rest."

She eyed Calhoun. At this point, she'd like to think he had something to do with all this. Of course, she had even less evidence of that than he had against Jimmy. "Two men came to Nick Raymond's ranch last night."

"To kill him?" Calhoun asked.

"That was their goal."

"I told you to get him back to Denver. I'm glad you finally listened." Seth narrowed his eyes on her. "I assume he's here with you?"

She nodded. "He came back with me. He's in Denver."

"But not here."

"No."

"How about the items Gayle Rodgers sent to Raymond's ranch? Toys? Papers? Did you bring them back with you?"

She nodded. With Calhoun involved, the last thing she wanted was to turn over the boxes. Not until she and Nick had a chance to go through their contents more thoroughly.

"Do you have them?"

"Not with me. Not here."

"Bring them in, then. Whatever is in them might fill in a few holes. And bring Raymond and his son with them. This attack in Wyoming is all the more reason they should be in protective custody."

Calhoun nodded, a little too eager for Melissa's liking.

Seth turned his probing frown on Calhoun for seemingly the first time since the meeting started. "It seems to me you have a lot left to prove. I want this kept under wraps until you can answer more of these questions with evidence."

"Will do."

Melissa let out a relieved breath. Once news of the investigation got out, no matter what she proved in the long run, Jimmy's name would always have a dark mark beside it in most people's minds. So maybe her arguments tonight had done some good. At least Seth had enough questions that he didn't feel comfortable going public with the investigation. At least Tammy wouldn't hear the rumors of an affair on top of everything else.

"Go ahead, Cory." Seth stood and ambled toward the door. "We're done here."

Melissa sat still and quiet until the door closed behind Calhoun. Seth settled back behind his desk, his gaze riveted to hers. "Where is Raymond now?"

She'd known this was coming, and she was braced for it. "He's in Denver, and he's willing to cooperate. But he doesn't trust our office or the police after what happened the last time his son was in our custody. And I have to say that until we find out how the gang knew where Jimmy was picking up Nick's son, I can't blame him."

"I'm sorry, Melissa. I can't leave this up to you alone." His voice held the tone of an adult talking down to a not-to-bright kid about what was best for him. "The fact that you are insisting on hiding them has me more than a little worried."

Melissa tried not to bristle. "What are you saying, Seth?"

"I know how you felt about Jimmy. I know what you're trying to do now." He spread his hands out on the desk blotter. "I'm afraid you're too personally involved in this to be objective."

No, no, no. She thought she was doing so well. She thought she was getting through to him. "Seth, stop. It's always personal, especially when it involves someone in law enforcement."

"Not like this is with you. Listen, I understand what you're going through. You and Jimmy Bernard were close. I get that. But as sorry as I am, I can't sit back and watch you try to undermine this office."

"Undermine? I'm not trying to undermine anyone. I'm trying to get to the truth."

"So is Cory Calhoun."

"Is he?"

"Yes."

She shook her head. "I don't buy it, Seth. From where I'm standing, I think he's out to get Jimmy." That was the truth of it. If nothing else, Calhoun seemed willing to warp any fact he could to besmirch Jimmy's name.

Seth canted his head to the side. "Melissa…"

She gritted her teeth. She hated when he took that

tone. "Calhoun's forcing evidence to fit his theory, Seth. He's convinced Jimmy was corrupt and he's grasping at anything he can to justify it. The question we should be asking is why would he do that?"

"Because he wants to get to the bottom of the situation? Because I asked him to be thorough? I know this whole thing is hard on Jimmy's wife, but we can't think about that. We have to know what Jimmy was into. We can't afford to tiptoe around hurt feelings. We can't afford to even appear as if we're willing to look the other way just because he was a police detective."

Appearances. That was it. Melissa should have seen it coming all along. "This is about your run for D.A."

"That has nothing to do with it."

"Yes, it does. You're willing to let Calhoun drive Jimmy's name into the ground so you can appear as if you aren't showing favoritism to police officers." She knew she was walking on thin ice talking to him like that, but she couldn't help it.

Seth tented his hands in front of his lips and studied her through narrowed eyes. He let out a heavy sigh and rubbed his forehead as if trying to ward off a headache. "You're off this case as of now, Melissa. I'm putting you on administrative leave. Turn in your identification and your weapon."

"This is bigger than politics, Seth."

"Damn right it is. It's about you losing all perspective." He reached out his hand, palm up, and cupped his fingers. "ID and gun."

She pulled out her identification with trembling fingers and laid it in his open hand. She removed her gun, unloaded the clip and checked the chamber and placed the pistol and ammunition on his desk.

"I'm sorry to have to do this to you, Melissa. But it's for the best."

Sure. The best. Whose best was the question.

"Now where are those boxes? And Raymond and his son?"

She raised her gaze and met her boss's eyes. "Sorry, Seth. I don't remember."

MELISSA'S HEAD WAS STILL buzzing when she left Seth's office. She walked through the halls, nodding and murmuring her hellos to coworkers, yet she barely saw them. She wasn't in any shape to talk to anyone right now. And God help her, if she ran into Calhoun milling around, waiting to rub in his victory, she wasn't sure what she'd do.

The slap of cool evening air felt good against her cheeks. The sun hadn't gone down yet, but streetlights lent a glow to the sidewalks, golden as the changing aspen leaves.

She took a deep breath and started winding along back streets toward the McDonald's where she'd left Nick and Jason. She tried not to dwell on Seth. She'd been stupid to think she could rely on his help. She was even more stupid to feel so betrayed now. She'd known he was eyeing a run for district attorney. Why she thought truth and justice would come before politics, she had no idea.

A shiver rippled up her spine. She glanced over her shoulder.

Two men walked twenty feet behind her. Dressed in

sloppy jeans, hoods pulled over their heads and hands stuffed in pockets, she couldn't see their faces. Worse yet, she couldn't see their hands. But she could read their body language just fine.

She wasn't sure how long they'd been behind her. If she hadn't been so rattled, she probably would have noticed them right away. They weren't trying for stealth. No, their goal was intimidation.

She tried to calm her breathing. More than anything, she wanted to break into a run. But she kept her pace steady and listened for any change coming from behind. She brought her hand to her hip, her fingers touching nothing but denim.

What a time to lose her gun.

Just ahead the side street came to a T. She turned to the right, away from the McDonald's, away from Nick and Jason. If these two were the men from last night, the last thing she wanted was to lead them straight to their prey.

"Hey."

She flinched at the sound of the voice.

"Why are you railroading José?"

The question was faint, barely audible above the traffic sounds coming from two streets over and wisps of theme music from a television show drifting from a window above. But it was obviously directed at her.

Her pulse pounded in her ears. She scanned the street. Mostly residential, there was no place she could run for help, not unless she wanted to drag an innocent resident into this mess. Of course even reaching a main thoroughfare wouldn't necessarily protect her. It hadn't helped Jimmy or Essie. The Latin Devils had taken them out right in broad daylight.

She slipped her hand into her purse and groped for her phone. Her fingers brushed wallet and sunglasses and lipstick. Had she left her phone in the truck?

"José, he didn't have nothing to do with that bitch dying. Nothing. Who are you covering up for?"

Melissa kept digging. The phone had to be here somewhere. It had to be. She took the next right and increased her pace.

"You running away from us? You can't run away." Their voices sounded closer, as if they too were walking faster, as if they were closing in. "You listening? You better listen, or we'll find other ways to show you we mean business."

"Lot of ways," said another voice.

She could hear the shuffle of rubber soles against concrete. Close behind. Too close. Her fingers closed over the phone's squarish shape.

She needed to buy some time. Even if she could get a call off to 911, it would take time for them to find her location. More time for a patrol car to arrive.

She slowed her steps, then stopped and turned to face them. She left her hand in her bag. She smoothed over the pad, trying to read the numbers with her fingertips.

The men stopped just five feet away, close enough for her to see their faces..

Were these the men who'd killed Jimmy? Who'd tried to kill Nick and Jason and her at the Circle J? She swept them with her eyes, trying to absorb every detail about them she could.

Hispanic males, both in their late teens to early twenties. Average height. Gang tats visible on their temples, cheeks and neck. Hands still in pockets, they stared at her in a way that was both wary and threatening. "The cops are lying. Jose didn't do nothing. You tell the DA that."

She located the nine. Skimming over the other numbers, she counted to the one and pressed it twice. "I just want to find the truth. That's all."

The larger of the two stepped toward her. Apparently comfortable enough to give up the wary and let the threatening take over his full focus. "You want the truth, you listen. The cops are lying."

She raised her chin and pushed as much bravado into her voice as she could muster. "Is that why you shot the detective? Because he was lying?"

"Detective?" The shorter one's voice cracked, apparently still struggling with puberty. "We didn't shoot no detective."

"Someone in the Latin Devils did."

The bigger one shook his head. "You don't know what you're talking about."

Somewhere a siren screamed.

She resisted the need to look over her shoulder. "I was there. There were four of you in the car. Two are now dead."

"You're crazy, lady. Whatever you're talking about, we had nothing to do with it."

"You didn't shoot Essie Castillo and Detective Bernard? The detective who arrested José Sanchez?"

"Hell no."

"Prove it."

"Prove it? Yeah, I'll prove it." The taller one pulled one hand from his pocket. With the flick of a wrist, the blade of a knife gleamed in the streetlight's warm glow.

Chapter Eleven

The first thing Nick saw when he rounded the street corner was the gleam of a knife's blade. A knife pointing straight at Melissa.

He brought his rifle to his shoulder. "Put the knife away, boys," he bellowed in a voice he reserved for cantankerous cattle and coyotes he caught skulking around his property.

The hoodlums spun around and stared at him. The one with the knife held it in front of him as if he thought he might be able to take Nick on.

"You really think that blade is going to help you here? Put it away." He lined up the knife man in his sights. When he'd seen the two follow Melissa into the side street, Nick had debated whether or not carrying the rifle through city streets was a wise move. Melissa was armed. She would surely take control before things got out of hand. But when he saw the knife in the man's fist and Melissa's hands empty, he knew something was wrong. And he was mighty glad he'd taken the risk. "Put it away right now."

The knife man folded his blade and stuffed his hand into his pocket.

"I want to see your hands. Both of you."

Slowly they did as he ordered.

Nick looked past them, focusing on Melissa. "Are these the guys?"

"You tell me." She glanced over her shoulder.

A siren screamed, the sound growing closer.

The two gang members glanced at each other. Then as one, they ran for an alley next to them.

Nick pulled his finger from the trigger guard and watched them go. He'd had enough shooting at people to last him eight lifetimes. He lowered the rifle.

Melissa headed straight for Nick. "What are you, crazy? Carrying a rifle down the street like that?" Her words were accusatory but her tone spoke only relief.

"Where's your gun?" Nick kept his eyes on the direction the two gang members had gone until he could no longer hear the smack of their sneakers on pavement.

"Were those the guys? The guys in the sedan? The ones who shot Jimmy and Essie?"

"No." He didn't have the slightest question in his mind. "What did they want?"

"You're sure these two weren't in that car?"

"I'm sure. What did they want?"

"I'll fill you in later."

"No, now."

She gestured up the street behind him. "Where's Jason?"

"He's locked in the truck, watching a movie." The little guy had run and climbed and slid until tired and cranky had taken him over. Desperate for quiet, Nick had taken him out to the truck, hoping a movie could lull him into a more quiet state. That's when he'd spotted

Melissa take her detour and head down the opposite street, two rough-looking teens following behind. He glanced back toward the truck. "I can see Jason from here."

She walked past him, heading for the truck.

He fell in beside her. "What did they want?"

"They wanted to tell me José Sanchez is innocent."

"And they pulled a knife to convince you?" Seemed like a bad move if you wanted to convince someone to trust you.

"They were lacking a bit in their powers of persuasion." A tremble behind her voice undercut the wryness of her humor and confidence of her stride. She was more shaken than she wanted him to believe.

He fought the urge to touch her. "You believe them?"

"I don't know what to believe." Melissa grabbed the door handle on the passenger side.

The siren wailed louder, closer.

Nick dashed around to the driver's side. If he wanted answers to his questions, he'd better hurry, because he sure wouldn't get them from the police.

JIMMY'S CABIN WAS ABOUT as fancy as the man himself. In other words, a dump. But even though Melissa had never been there before, it felt as familiar as an old friend's voice.

The outside wasn't the typical rustic-looking cabin constructed of rough-hewn lodgepole pine, not like Nick's ranch. Instead, it looked like it had been slapped together with plywood, duct tape and more than a little prayer.

Nick gave the door a hard shove with one hip to convince it to open. Jason raced inside.

Picturing a rat infestation, or worse, Melissa quickly stepped in behind him. The place was in order and housed no rodents that she could see. Probably thanks to Tammy's cleaning skills or the strong odor of mothballs that hung in the air.

Nick stepped in behind, hauling the suitcases they'd packed back at the ranch and following with the boxes. Once that was done, he scanned the single bedroom, the bathroom that sported a heavy plastic curtain instead of a door and the hot plate balanced on the dorm refrigerator and smiled. "I like it."

Melissa wasn't sure what there was to like for a person with no emotional attachment to the place or the owner, especially a man with a perfectly picturesque ranch like the Circle J. But she liked that he'd voiced approval of the dump anyway, even if it didn't make a lot of sense. "There's firewood in here already. If you start a fire, I'll spoon one of these casseroles into Tammy's Crock-Pot.

"Deal." He crossed to the little fireplace. Made of carefully laid stone, it was clearly the part of the cabin where Jimmy invested the most money and time. She remembered how many hours he'd spent building it stone by stone. She had no doubt that to Jimmy, this fireplace was as grand as Nick's at the Circle J. And the way Nick stood in front of it, one leg cocked while he studied the rock and nodded approvingly…it would have made Jimmy proud.

She tore her gaze from Nick and focused on the sad excuse for a kitchen. After all that had happened the past few hours, she was grateful to focus on something as normal and domestic as heating a casserole while her thoughts settled. She'd successfully fended off Nick's questions about her meeting with Seth and the whereabouts of her gun on the drive up. As long as she stayed busy now, she could continue to do so. And getting some distance from Nick, even if it was only across the room, was a bonus.

She needed to tell him all of it sometime. She knew that. But something was holding her back, something beyond the very awake and alert four-year-old now jumping on one of the twin beds. And she suspected it had a lot to do with her sorting through her own thoughts and feelings first.

She eyed the boxes Nick had set just inside the door. Now that she knew more about Calhoun's theories, the first thing she needed to do was take another look at Gayle's papers. Even the thought inspired a dread deep in her chest that she didn't want to face.

So she focused on heating dinner, and he built a fire. Soon they were warm and fed and Jason's eyelids were drooping over his big blue eyes.

Nick gestured to Melissa. "Want to tuck him in B-E-D?"

Melissa almost nodded but caught herself just in time. Nick was the boy's parent. Not her. Enabling him to duck the hard work of forging a relationship with his son would do neither him nor Jason any favors. And it would be just the opportunity she needed to get a peek at those papers alone. "I think you should this time."

"That doesn't usually go over well."

"You're not keeping your mind on the outcome you

want." She gave him a smile that she hoped was reassuring. "Besides, you two need to get some of these things worked out."

He blew a stream of air through puffed cheeks. "I suppose you're right."

He strode into the living room and knelt down to where Jason was playing with his superhero action figures. "Hey, Buddy. Do you want to bring these guys into bed with you?"

Jason stuck out his little chin. "Don't wanna go to bed."

"It's time. Now, do you want to bring your toys?"

"No."

Nick glanced in Melissa's direction. He got up and joined her next to the sink. "What am I doing wrong? It worked for you at the ranch."

"I don't wanna go to the ranch."

Nick stilled, as if bracing himself against the blow.

"I hate the ranch. I don't wanna go."

Melissa rinsed the last plastic plate from dinner and dried it with a ratty towel. She dropped her voice to a low whisper. "He knows that bothers you. That's all."

Nick focused on the little boy. "Time to go." He scooped him up and carried him to the little bedroom. He closed the door behind him, its paperlike thickness blocking little of Jason's mutiny scream.

Melissa pulled in a shaky breath and propped the box with Gayle's papers on one hip. Toting it to the old couch near the fireplace, she lowered herself onto a seat that hollowed out like a bucket beneath her and set the box between her knees. Nick had his challenges, she had hers.

She picked a folder out of the box and began sorting through the papers one more time. Soon Jason's protests stopped and she heard the low hum of Nick reading him a story. She flipped through one folder after the next. She had just located the file of charge card bills when Nick came back in the room.

"I have no idea if I did that right, but it's done."

"Sounded like it went okay." A nervous flutter stirred in the pit of her stomach as she fingered the folder's cover.

"What is it?"

"Nothing." She stared at the folder in her hand. "I know Jimmy didn't do any of the things Calhoun is accusing him of, yet…"

"You're worried about what you'll find inside?"

"Yeah."

"What can I help you with?" He reached out a hand for the folder in her lap.

She grabbed a folder she'd already been through and handed it to him instead.

"Phone records? Didn't we go over these back at the ranch?" He took it and sat on a recliner. Old springs creaked under his weight.

"I'm just making sure we didn't miss anything." She should just tell him about Calhoun's suspicions that Jimmy and Gayle were having an affair. But seeing that it was his ex-wife, that seemed like sensitive territory. And if she was being honest, she couldn't shake the feeling that saying it out loud would make it true.

She scooped in a deep breath and flipped open the cover of the credit card folder. The first thing she saw was a hotel charge.

Melissa's heartbeat accelerated. She eyed the hotel's address. The downtown Hilton, uncomfortably close to the Denver P.D.'s downtown station.

Nick let out a frustrated breath. "I don't see anything here that we didn't notice before."

"Keep looking." She flinched inwardly at the stress in her voice and flipped to the next page of charges. Sure enough. Another charge at the Hilton in the middle of the week. And another. She brought her fingers to her lips and closed her eyes.

"Melissa, what are you really looking for?"

Nick's voice gave her a jolt. She slapped her palm over the page of charges and opened her eyes.

He gave her a questioning look.

What was she doing? She must be losing her mind. She slid her hand off the side of the page. It was right in front of her in black and white. Saying it out loud wasn't likely to make things more real than that. "Gayle was charging hotel rooms in downtown Denver during the workweek."

He raised his brows but said nothing, just waited for her to continue.

She forced herself to tell him about Calhoun's theories, each word ripping a little piece of her away.

"So Gayle was having an affair with Detective Bernard? That's why the hotel rooms?" he said, joining the dots Melissa hadn't wanted to connect out loud. He seemed so calm about it. As if he was discussing a woman who was no more than a stranger to him.

"It's impossible."

He answered her with silence.

"Jimmy wouldn't. Not any more than he would take bribes."

Again, not a word.

"You don't believe me."

"People make mistakes, Melissa. Marriages fall apart for all kinds of reasons."

"Not Jimmy and Tammy's."

"How do you know that? You weren't part of it. Hell, I wasn't even fully aware that my own marriage was so far gone until…well, until Gayle really *was* gone." He thrust himself up from the recliner and took the spot on the couch next to her. "There might have been things happening that you didn't know about. Reasons Jimmy had for making choices that don't seem so smart once everything falls apart."

"You had an affair when you were married to Gayle?"

"No. Nothing like that."

"Then it's different."

He shrugged a shoulder. "Maybe. Maybe not. I never really gave our marriage a chance. Of course I didn't see it at the time, but I chose the ranch over Gayle long before she left. I probably shouldn't have been surprised when she finally chose the city over me."

It made sense. His desperation to sell his son on horseback riding. The stricken look that had crossed his face when Jason had said he hated the Circle J. "You're worried Jason will hate the ranch like Gayle did, that he'll leave you, too."

He looked down at the fire. "When you say it out loud, it sounds so stupid."

She let the papers fall loose on her lap. She had a

horrible urge to take him in her arms. To bring her lips to his like she had last night. To show him just how special she thought he was. "Your ranch is wonderful. It really is. But you know what?"

"Let me guess. I'm not my ranch?"

"You're even better." It was corny as hell, and she shouldn't have said it. It was as reckless and stupid as last night's kiss. But right then—after he'd admitted so much—she had to be honest. When she met him, she'd been drawn to the cowboy fantasy. But in the past few days, she'd grown to know him better. She'd come to see that the reality of Nick Raymond was far more seductive than any Stetson-wearing hero on a silver screen. And while she couldn't afford to let anything grow between them, she also could no longer pretend the feelings she had didn't exist.

He reached out and ran his fingers along her cheek. "You're something else, aren't you?"

She leaned her face into his touch. The feelings that had swamped her during their kiss welled inside, threatening to pull her under again. What she wouldn't give to forget everything and just let herself feel. Give herself over to that urge inside. Let herself go.

A jitter seized low in her chest. Not butterflies. Not warmth. Something dark and cold and unforgiving. Reaching up to her cheek, she took his hand in hers and cradled it safely in her lap. It was one of the hardest things she'd ever had to do. "I never understood my mother. Not until now."

His brows dipped low over his eyes. "Your mother?"

Melissa nodded. She knew it seemed like a non

sequitur. To her, the leap from this out-of-control need to her mother was as natural as breathing. "She was the most carefree person I've ever known. And the most dependent."

"On you?"

"On men."

"Boyfriends?"

"One after another. She was beautiful. Men liked her. Good thing. I don't think she could have survived without a man. Not physically. Not emotionally." She could feel him watching her, probably trying to figure out where in the world she was coming from, but she didn't dare look up into his eyes. She just focused on his hands, rubbing her fingertips over thick calluses and square nails.

"That had to be mighty hard on you."

"Some of her boyfriends weren't the best of men."

"They hurt you?"

She shook her head. That would probably make sense to him. That she didn't want to get involved because she'd been abused. She'd been lucky. And when she'd felt any kind of leer or threat from one of her mother's men, she'd tried not to stick around. "I ran away a lot. Waited for the booze to wear off, waited for my mother to find another man. Waited until I was picked up by the cops. Only one time when I was brought back, my mother was no longer there."

"What happened?"

"She was killed. Murdered by her boyfriend."

He turned the tables on her, this time, rubbing his fingers over hers, cupping her hands with his. "I'm sorry."

"Don't be. Not for me, anyway. The guy who brought me back that time was an officer named Jimmy Bernard. And he changed my life."

He nodded, as if he understood her bond with Jimmy. "He was there when you needed him."

"And he never left." She tried to swallow, but her throat was too thick to function. Funny she could talk about her mother's tragic death without batting an eye, but even good things about Jimmy…they were just too close. "Jimmy was the only one I could count on, you know?"

"And now you're not sure."

The room blurred into a watery mosaic of color. She opened her eyes wide so the tears wouldn't break free. She didn't want to admit it, that her belief in Jimmy had been shaken. She didn't want to even think it, let alone say it out loud.

"What else happened in that meeting tonight, Melissa? Where is your gun?"

"Seth put me on administrative leave."

"Administrative leave?"

"I'm suspended. I had to turn in my ID and gun." She looked down at the tangle of their fingers. "I don't have any legal authority and I'm unarmed."

"Why didn't you tell me right away?"

"I don't know. I needed to get used to the idea myself first, I guess."

"And did that work?"

She didn't even bother shaking her head. "I can't protect you anymore. You were right all along. Coming back wasn't such a good idea."

He shook his head. "I can't take Jason back to the ranch. Not until those men are caught."

"So go somewhere else. Anywhere else. Just until this all blows over."

"And when will that happen?"

"I don't know."

His lips flattened into a line, and he stared into the fire. "And if I did that, just went somewhere, what would you do?"

She pulled herself up. "Jimmy was there for me when I needed him most. I have to be there for him."

Nick's lips flattened into a line. "If things change, our plans will have to change with them. But for now, I don't see any reason to change anything. You'll be there for Jimmy, and I'll be here for you."

A spot beneath her throat hollowed out and for a moment, she couldn't speak. When she recovered her voice, it sounded thin and weak. "You don't need to save me."

"Who said anything about saving?"

"You weren't thinking that? After what happened on the street tonight?"

"I didn't save you out there. I simply had your back." He canted his head to the side. "And a handy hunting rifle."

She wanted to smile at that last bit. She needed to smile, make light of this. But somehow, she just didn't have it in her. "I can't."

"You need someone you can rely on, and I'm here. It doesn't have to mean any more than that. That's all there needs to be."

She shook her head. "I still...I can't."

"Why not?'

"Because what if I do rely on you, and then you're not there?" Like her mother. Like Seth. Maybe even like Jimmy. It was the fear that had always gnawed at the back of her mind, ever since she was a kid. And no matter what answer Nick gave her, she knew he couldn't make it go away.

Chapter Twelve

When Nick awoke the next morning, mired in the lumpiest couch on the planet, the last thing he expected to find was no Melissa. And no truck.

He leaned against the doorjamb, the cool morning air raising chills over his skin. Obviously she'd been serious about not relying on him last night.

Pajama feet shuffled across the floor behind him. "Where did Melissa go?"

Good question. He closed the cabin's front door and turned to face his son. No doubt he'd have even more of a problem with Melissa's absence than Nick did. He braced himself for the disappointment and the inevitable battle over breakfast food. "She had some errands to run. I guess you're stuck with me."

Jason nodded, as if it wasn't a big deal.

Huh. No complaints? Maybe they were making progress after all. Now for the next hurdle. "Should we see what there is for breakfast?"

"I want to play."

"Play while I get breakfast."

"I want to play with you."

At first, Nick wasn't sure he understood. His son

wanted to play, he got that. But he actually said he wanted to play with Nick? As his shock wore off, he registered Jason's stare, waiting for an answer. To hell with breakfast. "That sounds like a lot of fun, Jason. Let's do it." Apparently *something* had changed last night. Maybe not with Melissa, but something had changed between him and his son.

He followed Jason to the fireplace. The little guy plunked down on the floor and set his Spider-Man action figure on the stone hearth. "My guy is climbing this."

"Where's my guy?"

Jason pointed to a blue Power Ranger laying on the floor. "He's your guy, but he's not in charge."

"Is your guy in charge?"

"He's Spider-Man."

"Okay." He guessed that answered that, though he wasn't sure how. He picked up the blue ranger and mimicked Jason's movements, making the toy climb the side of the hearth.

Jason watched him. He scratched his chin, the little crease in the center so much like Nick's own.

"What is it, Buddy?" Nick asked.

Little eyebrows scrunched low over serious eyes. "There's a big problem."

A big problem, huh? Nick couldn't wait to hear this. "What's the problem?"

"I don't have a horse. Your guy needs to ride a horse."

Nick smiled. So the blue Power Ranger was a rancher. He should have known. He nodded at Spider-Man. "What about your guy?"

Jason looked down at the plastic man in his hand. When he glanced back up at Nick, he paused for a moment, then bobbed his head up and down. "My guy needs a horse, too."

MELISSA COULD HEAR NICK'S words of the night before echoing in her ears louder than the roar of construction equipment remodeling the county jail. *You need someone you can rely on, and I'm here. It doesn't have to mean any more than that. That's all there needs to be.*

The problem was, it *did* mean more than that. She'd been awake half the night, her mind whirring with all the things that it meant, a list that seemed to grow with each day.

She had no business feeling the way she felt about Nick. She'd only known him a few days. Yet there it was. This feeling. This need. Budding inside her like a spring flower. And she was so afraid to trust that it was real, let alone rely on it to grow.

She passed through security, smiling and sharing a few words with the deputy at the metal detector. Everything was different at the jail. Everything either torn up or detoured into an area it didn't belong. She felt lost. But not nearly as lost as when she concentrated on her own thoughts. Took note of her own feelings.

It doesn't have to mean any more than that. That's all there needs to be.

Did he feel anything more? Want anything more? She thought so. When she caught him looking at her, she was sure there was something there, something as strong as the feelings that clamored inside of her. But when he wasn't next to her, she wondered if she made the whole thing up.

She held a cool hand against her forehead. Did any of it even matter?

She couldn't do this. It had nothing to do with Nick, and yet it had everything to do with him. Around him she felt so vulnerable, like he'd opened a wound inside her that would never quite heal.

She threaded through the detoured corridors, her heels clacking on the waxed tile floor. There was only one answer. Nick and Jason had to go back to the ranch. And it was up to her to do whatever she could to make sure they were safe enough to do so.

She reached the area where lawyers visited their clients. The place was oddly cheery, in a bland, government-building sort of way. The upbeat jangle of music from the local forecast of the Weather Channel bounced off concrete and tile.

A deputy ushered her into one of the meeting rooms. The room was little bigger than a phone booth and smelled of body odor, floor wax and a faint hint of the ever-present construction dust hanging like an invisible fog in the air. In front of a Plexiglas window, a stainless-steel counter stretched, a stool bolted to the floor beneath it. The setup was the same on the other side. Telephones were attached to the wall by a short cable on either side of the shatterproof glass. She perched on the hard plastic seat and waited for José Sanchez.

Sanchez was shorter than she remembered, barely five foot five, but he carried himself like he was twice the size. Shoulders back and chin held at a haughty angle, he peered at her as if upset she'd interrupted his day. He lowered himself onto the bench on his side of the window and stared at her a good long while before picking up the phone.

She picked up her phone as well and held it to her ear.

"You with the D.A.'s office?"

She'd expected some type of Hispanic accent, but his words sounded as flatly Midwestern as if he'd grown up on a farm in Kansas. Strange to think that she'd been working on the case against him, and yet she'd never spoken to him until now. She'd never even seen his face, except in his booking photo. "My name is Melissa Anderson. I'm an investigator with the district attorney's office."

"My lawyer said you might be trying to trick me into talking with you."

"I'm not on the job anymore. I'm suspended. I'm here as a private citizen." Of course if Seth knew she was here, he'd wish he'd given her a pink slip instead of administrative leave.

"Whatever. I don't got to talk to you. Not without my lawyer."

"I don't need you to talk. Just listen."

"Okay. Why not?" He plunked an elbow on the counter as if settling in for the duration. His gaze drifted down toward her chest.

She resisted the urge to button her blouse another notch. His leer was meant to intimidate, to make her uncomfortable, and she wouldn't give him what he wanted. Besides, it wasn't going to be easy to sell a lie to a practiced liar. She was going to have to give the performance of her life. If her nonexistent cleavage and not-very-sexy uniform of blouse and blazer distracted him enough to keep him from spotting the lie, she might as well use it to her advantage.

She leaned forward an inch. "I'd like to go over some theories with you."

"Knock yourself out."

"The D.A.'s office thinks you were bribing police officers."

"Now why would I do that?"

"To be specific, they think you were bribing Detective Bernard."

Sanchez stretched his mouth open in an exaggerated yawn.

"They think you killed Gayle Rodgers because she was informing the district attorney about the bribes."

That got his attention. He straightened, intense brown eyes drilling into her. "I didn't kill no one."

"That's not all." She paused. "Four members of your gang shot and killed Detective Bernard and a victims' rights advocate two days ago."

"I told you, I didn't kill no one. And I didn't tell no one to kill no one, either."

Right. She couldn't count the number of times defendants proclaimed their innocence. It was a line each of them might as well have tattooed to their forehead along with the myriad of gang ink each one sported.

"Two of those same friends of yours—"

"Who says they're my friends?"

"Sorry, members of your gang."

He tilted his head. "I'm not part of any gang."

"Fine. But these four men are members of the Latin

Devils. Or, I should say, two of them are. The other two are dead."

"Lady, you don't know what the hell you're talking about."

"I was there. Two of the men attempted to murder a witness to the shooting of Detective Bernard. They crashed into a ravine. I know what I'm talking about, since I helped them do it."

Sanchez shook his head. "Whatever. Not that. I don't know about that."

Right. "I'm sure their mothers would like to give them funerals. But we don't have any names."

"And you think I know their names?"

"Yeah, I think you just might."

"And why's that? Because we Latinos, we all know each other?"

"Because you and the four men I'm talking about are all Latin Devils."

"You're crazy, lady."

Her turn to throw that "whatever" back at him. She leaned toward the Plexiglas, planting elbows on stainless steel. "I'm doing you a favor, José. Giving you a gift. So listen up."

He heaved a sigh and dropped his eyes once again.

"Our witness can't identify the two Latin Devils who are still alive. There's no reason for them to risk going after him again. We've got nothing on them. The police have nothing. They're off the hook. Understand?"

Sanchez let out a scoff. "I understand perfect. You're the one who don't understand. These gang members you say shot the detective, they weren't no Latin Devils."

"Right. Just make sure you tell them—"

"Didn't you hear me? They ain't Latin Devils. I ain't saying I'm part of the gang or nothing. But I hear stuff, even in here. The usual gossip. You know? Who is part of what. Who does what. And I can tell you there ain't no way anyone in the Latin Devils killed no police detective. And they didn't try to kill some witness, either."

"Why should I believe you?"

"I don't care if you believe me or not." He shrugged again, gesturing with his free hand as he talked into the phone. "It don't have anything to do with me. I still don't see why you're telling me this stuff in the first place."

Was he just playing with her for entertainment? She had to admit it was a possibility. Even a probability. Her best bet was to make her point and pray he got the message through to the rest of the gang. "No one will ever be able to prove who killed Detective Bernard. The witness is no longer a threat."

Sanchez bobbed his head and rolled his eyes, mocking her. "And you think I can call off the Latin Devils, save this witness some pain?"

"And maybe save your friends a prison sentence, too. Think of that."

"I told you, they're not my friends."

"Yes, yes, I know." She was tired of Sanchez's games, tired of being jerked around by a hoodlum. "Will you make sure they know the witness can't identify them? Will you pass that along?"

"Maybe I could and maybe I couldn't *if* these four were Latin Devils. They ain't. So I can't really do a thing for you, can I?"

She leaned her forehead on the heel of one hand. He had to be lying. Didn't he? It was what men like José Sanchez did. "The D.A.'s investigator on the case says they are Latin Devils. Who am I supposed to believe? You or him?"

"Me." Sanchez pointed to a series of tattoos that marked his face from temple to neck. "Your cop killers, they have marks like these?"

She remembered Nick mentioning tattoos in his original statement to police, but he'd never given her a detailed description. "Those mark them as Latin Devils?"

Sanchez smiled. "*Something* like these. Not saying I'm in a gang."

He didn't have to say it. She knew he was. "Mind if I take a picture?" She pulled out her cell phone.

"The cops have my mug shots. You want one for your own use?" He sent another leer down to her chest.

"Yeah, whatever." She snapped a few pictures of the side of his face. "I'm going to have a chat with Detective Marris from the gang bureau, too, José. Just so you know."

He leaned back on his stool. "You do that. He'll tell you the same as me."

"If this is a line of B.S., you'll be hearing from me."

"Should've told me that before." He lowered one lid in a wink. "I would have enjoyed another visit. Only next time, wear something sexy."

NICK HAD JUST FINISHED some of the most imaginative, expansive and exhausting action-figure adventures he'd ever known when the door to the little cabin swung open and Melissa stepped inside.

"Melissa!" Jason leaped up from the fireplace and scampered across the floor.

She flung her arms wide and engulfed him in a hug. "Did you guys have fun today?"

Jason beamed up at her. "Daddy and I played that our guys were on a ranch. They were exploring mountains." He pointed to the fireplace.

Nick was still caught on the word *daddy*.

Melissa met his gaze across the room. She smiled, as if she'd noticed, too. "It sounds like you and your daddy had a blast."

Jason squirmed out of her hug. Grabbing her hand, he pulled her toward the fireplace. "I'll show you. You can have a guy, too. 'Cept I don't have any girl guys."

"Wait, Jason." Melissa gathered him toward her and knelt down. "I have to talk to your daddy for a minute. Then you can show me the guys. Okay?"

"Okay." He let go of her hand and returned to the fireplace.

Melissa stepped toward the kitchen end of the room and motioned for Nick to follow.

He joined her, leaning one hip on the sink in a posture much more relaxed than he felt. Before she told him her piece, he had a question he needed to ask. "Where were you?"

She paused, as if she wasn't certain she wanted to tell him. Finally she met his eyes. "Jail."

"Jail?" He narrowed his eyes, hurriedly shifting the pieces into place in his mind. He had a feeling she didn't mean behind bars. At least not her. "You visited José Sanchez?"

She nodded.

"Why did you have to see him?" He tried to make the question sound light, as if he was merely curious, but his tone sounded more like aggressive interrogation.

"I wanted to find out a little more about the Latin Devils."

"And you couldn't just talk to one of the gang bureau detectives?"

"Not about this."

"Isn't a guy like that dangerous?"

"It's my job. I have to deal with guys like that all the time. Who do you think gets prosecuted by the D.A.?"

She was right. What in the hell had gotten into him? He was being ridiculous, trying to protect a woman who didn't want his protection, didn't need it, and wasn't his to protect.

And never would be.

He heaved a deep breath. Time to start over. Try to stay sane this time. Focus only on things that concerned him. "What did you ask him about? The men who followed you last night?"

"That didn't come up."

If that hadn't, he knew what did. "The men who shot Jimmy."

She nodded. "I told him our witness couldn't identify the two who were still living."

"You…what?" He could see what she was doing. Trying to make it possible for him to return to the ranch with Jason. A goal he would be happy about, thrilled about really, if only it hadn't come hard on the heels of their discussion last night. Now he saw it for what it was. Not Melissa trying to give him his life back, but Melissa pushing him away.

He glanced at Jason, busy making Spider-Man climb the fireplace's rock wall. If he'd ever needed a reminder of his priorities, this morning had been it. He needed to keep Jason's best interest foremost in his thoughts. Jason's and his own. "Good thinking. If they don't know I can identify them, I'm not a threat. Jason and I can go back to the Circle J."

She didn't answer, just canted her gaze to the side, focusing on a spot just off his right shoulder.

"Did Sanchez buy your story?" he asked.

"He says the men who shot Jimmy and Essie weren't Latin Devils."

"Of course he's going to say that."

"That was my reaction, too. But he insisted. Said no Latin Devils killed Jimmy and no Latin Devils were gunning for witnesses."

Nick shook his head. He could guess the rest. "And he said that he's innocent, too."

"Yes."

"Isn't that the way it always works with these guys?"

"Usually, yes."

"But you believe him?" He knew she was desperate for evidence that Jimmy hadn't taken bribes or had an affair. And after the credit card records had proved Calhoun's theories more than disproved them, she might be grasping at anything that went against Calhoun's version of events. But he was still surprised she'd buy the story of a man like José Sanchez. The man who killed Gayle.

"I don't know what I believe." She reached into her bag. "I need you to take a look at something for me."

"Me? You're really asking for my help this time?"

She gave him a frown, still not quite meeting his eyes.

He knew he should keep his personal disappointment out of this. She certainly hadn't promised him anything. There wasn't anything more between them than a single kiss. There never could be.

He took off his hat and set it down on the tiny kitchen table. "What do you need me to look at?"

She fished her cell phone out of her purse. She hit a few buttons and handed it to him.

He looked down at the phone and focused on a photo of the side of a man's face. The image was a little distorted, as if shot through some kind of glass. The reflection of lights blocked out part of the man's shaved head.

"See the tattoos?"

How could he miss them? Thick black lines met with more intricate swirls, marking the sides of the man's face, his head and his neck. Every mark both art in a visual sense and profanity for what he knew it stood for. "These look like the ones on the guys who followed you last night. I'm not sure they're exactly the same, though, since they were wearing hoods. I didn't see all of the tattoos."

"How about the guys who killed Jimmy?" She pointed to a button on the phone. "I have more than one shot. Another might give you a better angle."

He flicked through all the photos on the phone. Different angles, same effect. Finally he looked up at Melissa.

This time her eyes met his. "So? Are these the same tattoos as the ones on the men in the sedan?"

He wasn't sure what she wanted him to say, but he had no doubts about what he'd seen. "No. They're totally different."

Chapter Thirteen

Melissa gathered her hair and lifted it off the back of her neck, some tendrils already damp with sweat. The sun hovered low in the sky, just barely over the mountains in the west. But its heat beat down, the thin air doing little to mitigate its rays. Pine rose on the hillside, its sharp spears thrusting skyward, its clean smell nearly covering the odor of stale beer wafting from a nearby Dumpster. Cigarette butts littered a patch of gravel that formed an employee parking lot.

They'd parked down the street and walked just to be safe, not sure what they'd find. The spot on the outskirts of the metro area wasn't *rural,* not in the way that Nick might define rural. But it felt isolated to her. A lot of pine forest and dry hillsides dotted with houses and the occasional cluster of businesses. And she found it a little strange that Detective Marris had designated it as the place to meet.

She supposed she should be grateful he'd agreed to meet them alone at all. She'd made him agree not to take Nick and Jason in on the material-witness warrant. He didn't seem overly concerned about looking the other way. He didn't seem to care at all. But she had to wonder if he chose the meeting spot so no one would see them together.

Marris climbed out of his unmarked car and strode across the lot, shoes crunching on gravel. A tall, beanpole of a man, Marris had the friendliest smile she'd ever seen. But underneath his sunny exterior, Melissa had always sensed a will that was hard as diamonds. Jimmy had respected Marris. She'd found it impossible not to follow suit.

Marris greeted Nick and kidded around with Jason for a couple of seconds, then he turned to her. "So what you got for me?"

She offered him her cell.

He took the phone and studied the image. After a second or two he looked up at her, peering over his sunglasses. "Is this a quiz?"

"Please, Ben. It's important."

"I sure hope so. I didn't come all this way to be quizzed on trivia. It's a picture of José Sanchez."

"His tattoos. What can you tell me about them?"

His gaze flicked to the phone and back to her. He paused as if waiting for her to deliver some kind of punch line. "Most of them are pretty standard for a member of the Latin Devils. Is that what you're looking for?"

That was precisely what she was looking for. "Do all Latin Devils have tattoos like these?"

"Some of them." A teacher's tone replaced his suspicion that she was trying to punk him. He pointed to the digital image. "Especially these on the side of Sanchez's head. See these lines and the devil's tail? Each member gets these when they're initiated."

"So if someone doesn't have those tattoos, they don't belong to the Latin Devils?"

"Nope." He glanced up. "Are you going to tell me why all the questions?"

"Because that's what José Sanchez told me. That all Latin Devils have these tattoos."

His brows arched. "So he *can* actually tell the truth. Who knew?"

Melissa glanced at Nick. He'd been standing on the edge of the conversation, watching Jason who was now exploring a collection of pine saplings at the edge of the parking area.

Nick nodded to her and cleared his throat. "The men who shot Detective Bernard had different tattoos."

"You're sure?"

"Absolutely."

Ben Marris narrowed his eyes on Nick. "I've been wanting to ask you about that. I noticed the tatts in the police sketch, they were different. I was wondering if the artist got the tatts mixed up. Or if you just didn't remember."

"I remember lines, but they were different. And no devil's tail. They aren't like these." Nick pointed to Melissa's phone.

"So that would mean the Latin Devils aren't the ones who killed Jimmy and Essie?" Melissa looked to Marris for a verdict she knew was coming. A drip of sweat trickled down her back.

"Appears not. No."

"Are they tatts a different gang might wear?" Nick asked.

Marris gave his head a brief shake. "Judging by what I saw in the sketches, they're not part of any gang."

Melissa frowned. She wasn't following him. "What do you mean?"

"Just that. They're not Latin Devils. And they're not anything else, either. Not any gang I know, and I know them all. The ones operating in this area, anyway. My guess? They're wannabes. Guys who play at being in a gang. Guys who want to appear tough but don't really belong to anything."

She mulled that over in her mind. "Are they just kids?"

"Maybe. You see that kind of thing in the suburbs sometimes. Guys who are working up the nerve to try the real thing. Or they could be just operating in their own interest. Hard to tell."

Nick held up a finger. "But if they're kids, there might be missing person reports for the two killed in the mountains. Right? Parents missing their sons?"

Marris tilted his head to the side. "Maybe."

Melissa didn't want to think of the two who had died in the crash as someone's son, someone's brother, some lost kid trying to find his way. Thinking of them as gang members had been easier. As if they weren't real people then. As if gang members didn't have parents or siblings or anyone to mourn them.

Her face felt hot, the skin tight. "Have you told anyone about the tattoos? Who the kids might be?"

"I included the apparent discrepancy in the tattoos in my report," Marris answered.

A report Calhoun had probably seen. A report he'd

apparently ignored, or at the very least, hadn't studied closely. "Have you talked to Cory Calhoun directly?"

"About the tattoos? I've talked to him plenty."

"What did he say?"

"What could he say? I told you on the phone, Calhoun's on a witch hunt. He's ignoring facts left and right."

He didn't have to tell her that, after she sat through the meeting last night. But now things were different. Now they were unraveling Calhoun's theory. "Can you take this to Seth Wallace? Tell him about the tattoos? Calhoun's story doesn't hold together if it isn't the Latin Devils who killed Jimmy. Maybe more of it doesn't hold together, either. Maybe none of it does."

"Wouldn't surprise me. Calhoun is more concerned with revenge than anything else."

Nick's eyebrows flicked upward. "Against who? Jimmy Bernard?"

"You got it."

Melissa frowned. She'd had plenty of misgivings about Calhoun, but she thought his attitude was based on ambition. He'd smelled Jimmy's blood in the water and wanted to be first in line for the feeding frenzy. It hadn't occurred to her there might be more to it. "What kind of grudge?"

"Jimmy wrote up Calhoun years ago, back when he was Calhoun's supervisor in the P.D. Don't remember what Calhoun did—not important—but the whole thing hurt his career. It was the reason he jumped at the D.A. job."

It made sense. The way Calhoun was shoehorning

facts to fit his Jimmy-is-dirty theory had the vehemence behind it that fit best with a personal grudge.

"And then there's Seth Wallace."

"Seth?"

"A guy like Calhoun brings up the possibility of dirt in the police department, and a political animal like Wallace is going to do one of two things. He's going to either sweep it under the rug, or if he can't, he'll crucify anyone he can find and call it the even hand of justice."

Melissa thought of Seth's reaction to Calhoun in his office. The investigator had little evidence to back up anything he was saying, yet Seth let him continue anyway. At the same time, he ordered him to keep the investigation quiet as death. Covering himself both ways. "So what are you saying? We shouldn't point the tattoos out to Seth?"

"No we should. *You* should. But don't expect him to do a whole hell of a lot about it. Not until he has definitive proof that the investigation is crap, the story leaks to the press, or he wins the election."

So in the meantime, the P.D. was out looking for the two remaining Latin Devils who shot Jimmy and Essie, and yet they didn't really exist. Melissa glanced at Nick, at Jason playing at the edge of the parking lot.

In the meantime, Nick and Jason had nowhere to go.

WALKING BACK TO THE TRUCK, Nick couldn't explain the strange prickle at the back of his neck. He twisted around to look behind them. Pine and a few golden shocks of aspen mixed with a smattering of houses and businesses lining the street. Cars buzzed along the nearby highway. A normal day happening all around them. Yet he felt nothing close to normal.

Maybe it was that meeting with Detective Marris. Or the strained silence that had fallen between Melissa and him since their discussion the night before. But whatever it was, he wanted this unsettled feeling to stop. He wanted to know what was coming next.

He glanced at Melissa. She looked straight ahead as she walked, but he could feel she was aware of his stare. "Some of the things Detective Marris said. They don't add up."

"Like what?"

He shrugged, trying to put his misgivings into words. "Maybe four kids from the suburbs would know how to shoot assault rifles, I don't know. God knows if they were any good at shooting, I wouldn't be here. But…"

She glanced his way. "It seems like a stretch."

"Exactly." He let out a breath. Maybe that was his problem. The strain between the two of them. A brief glance from her, an acknowledgment of his hunch, and his chest felt less tight. The unease at the back of his neck lessened ever so slightly. "Besides those guns are expensive."

"It would depend on the family the young men came from."

"Which at the very least should give the police another lead when it comes to identifying them."

"He also said they might not be affiliated with any group."

"That theory makes more sense to me. But it begs the question of why they are involved in this at all."

She nodded an encouragement to go on.

"How did a few wannabe gang members decide to pick off a police detective on the street in broad daylight? Why would they do it? And how did they know he'd be there?"

"The leak." The skin around her eyes looked tight. Lines dug on either side of her mouth.

"It's hard for you, isn't it? To think someone in the system is behind this?"

"The whole thing is hard for me. I still want to believe it never happened."

"What if it wasn't Jimmy who was the target? What if it was the woman who was also killed?"

"Essie?" She shook her head. "She's a victim's advocate. She's only been with the D.A. for a few months."

"What if she's tied to the men in the car? What if they knew where to find her because *she* told them? What if it's something personal?"

"You're saying it has nothing to do with Gayle."

"We just assumed it did."

"Everyone assumed it." She looked straight into his eyes, her face alive, the air almost vibrating around her. "I can't believe I didn't see that possibility before. I can't believe it didn't even occur to me."

"Sometimes it helps to have an outside point of view. Of course, we don't really know—"

"But it's worth looking into." She nodded, her step a little faster, a little spring to it that wasn't there before.

His chest swelled a little at the thought that he'd had some role in putting that spring there.

She looked up at him. "Thanks for your help…with the tattoos and the ideas."

"You don't have to thank me. You know that."

"No, I do. Last night, you offered to help and I…" She shook her head.

"It doesn't need to be more than it is."

She pressed her lips into a hint of a smile. "I know. You said that last night, too. And I appreciate it."

He smiled back at her, but he had no idea how he managed it. Because although he said what was between them didn't have to be more, more was exactly what he wanted.

She broke the eye contact first and jammed her hand into her bag. "I need to call Seth." She pulled out her cell phone and punched a few buttons.

Nick hugged Jason's little body tighter against his shoulder and focused on the road ahead. The truck was only a short distance away. He had to start thinking about unlocking the doors and strapping Jason into his seat. But even so, he found himself holding his breath just a little, waiting to hear the mellow tones of Melissa's voice as she talked on the phone.

Instead he heard the burned rubber screech of tires on pavement. A scream ripped from Melissa's lips.

Nick looked up just in time to see an SUV barreling straight for them.

Chapter Fourteen

Nick didn't stop to think. Clamping Jason tight to his shoulder with one arm, he grabbed Melissa with the other and dove for the ditch.

An engine roared behind them, bearing down.

Nick let go of Melissa and shot out a hand to break his and Jason's fall. He crashed to rocky dirt. The force of his fall shuddered through his arm and into his body. Rock jammed into the heel of his hand. Something cracked. His arm gave and he collapsed to his side, barely avoiding smashing Jason between his body and the ground.

Jolted awake, Jason cried out in his ear.

The sound of the engine roared above them. It sounded bigger than an SUV. A Hummer? A damn tank?

Nick scrambled to get his feet under him. The rocky soil was parched and loose, sparse grass slick as ice under his boots. He reached for the spot where Melissa had been and grasped nothing but air. "Melissa!"

"Here."

He followed the voice. He could see her blond hair, glowing against the green backdrop of young pine.

The engine revved from above. Gravel sprayed under tire treads.

His boots found purchase. He scrambled forward, reaching with his free hand to help Melissa. Pain razored through his arm. He lurched forward, dizzy.

She was beside him. Helping him. Pulling him.

His vision cleared just as they hit the edge of the trees. He gritted his teeth and pushed forward, through the tangle of brush at the edge of the forest and into the cool, sparse understory.

Behind them the engine's roar sounded different. Spinning around, he peered through the trees. A red SUV bumped back onto the road. It bolted down the street and disappeared.

"Daddy!"

He held the little body tight. "Jason. Buddy. Are you okay?" He pulled back to examine his son.

Except for a few scratches on his arms, he seemed fine.

Nick scanned Melissa. "Are you okay?"

She nodded and leaned hands on knees, trying to catch her breath. Hair clung to a scrape on her cheek. But underneath it all, she still had that fierce hold on control he'd witnessed the moment he met her. She looked up at him. "You're hurt."

Jason reached for Nick's free hand. "You need a Band-Aid."

Nick glanced down at his hand, hanging limply at his side. Blood oozed from scrapes and cuts on his palm, but that was the least of his problems. Now that the adrenaline of the panicked moment was draining away, a bone-deep ache pulsed up his arm.

"It's broken, isn't it?" Melissa reached out like Jason had, stopping short of touching him.

"We need to get back to the cabin."

"You should go to a hospital. Have it set."

"I'm fine. Might Jimmy have some kind of first-aid kit?"

"I can guarantee it. But a hospital would be better."

"Can't be helped. We need to get to the cabin. We'll decide what to do from there."

Melissa slipped one arm around his back and the other around him and Jason both. "You saved my life."

He looked down at her. He wished he could raise his hand, smooth Melissa's silken hair back from her cheek, cradle her sweet face and claim her lips. Let her know that everything was okay. As long as she and Jason were alive, unhurt…everything was fine.

For the fourth time in as many days, he'd come too close to losing those he loved. Jason and…

The realization shuddered through him like the shock waves of a bomb.

That was it, wasn't it? Jason wasn't the only one he loved. Despite having been down this path before. Despite knowing she would never be happy spending her life with him. Despite promising himself he wouldn't go there. He'd fallen for Melissa Anderson.

Now what the hell was he going to do?

MELISSA WAS STILL SHAKING when she finally got in touch with Seth on the drive back to Jimmy's cabin. She'd let Nick drive, giving into his insistence despite what she was sure was a broken arm. Now she watched the lines of pain etching his face in the dashboard's glow as he steered with one hand, the other lying still in his lap, her cell phone clapped to her ear.

Not knowing how long service would last in this mountainous terrain, she filled Seth in on her visit with Sanchez, her meeting with Marris, and Nick's observations about the shooters and the possibility of Essie being their real target. But despite showing strong interest in Nick's alternate theory, Seth's main focus seemed to be Marris.

"What did the detective tell you?"

"A few things. About Calhoun. About his history with Jimmy. About how his whole investigation might be based more on revenge than evidence."

"That's funny."

"Funny? I'd call it a lot of things, but funny isn't one."

Seth chuckled, though she hadn't meant the comment as humorous. "You don't know what I know about Marris."

She'd had enough revelations about other people to last the rest of her life. She wasn't sure she could handle another. She took a deep breath. "What is it?"

"It wasn't just Jimmy Bernard who was taking money from the Latin Devils."

"Marris was." She couldn't believe it. She stared out the window at the tops of trees rushing by as they left the city outskirts behind and climbed into the mountains. It seemed everyone she respected, everyone she trusted…she shook her head. "Can you prove it this time, Seth?"

"We have a lot more evidence against Marris. He was the original target of this investigation, before we knew Jimmy was involved. If it wasn't for Gayle Rodgers and then Jimmy getting killed, Marris would already be charged."

Was it possible? Could Marris be the one who was lying? And if so, how far did that lying go? Was he the one who told those gangster wannabes where to find Jimmy? Did he pay them to take out a friend in order to save his own hide? Was Marris or his remaining two hit men behind the wheel of that SUV?

She knew she was jumping to conclusions. She didn't know what Calhoun had on Marris. It could be twice what he had on Jimmy, and that still wouldn't add up to much.

She had to get things straight if she was going to figure out what to do next. "What about Calhoun? Did Jimmy write him up, damage his career?"

"That part is true."

"Why didn't you tell me that before?"

"It has nothing to do with the investigation."

"How can you say that? It has to color his view of Jimmy."

"It was a long time ago, Melissa. Calhoun's career is back on track. Everything's going well for him. Why would he risk it all now to get revenge against a dead man?"

He had a point. Still she sensed a rabidness in Calhoun that would be perfectly explained by a personal grudge. "Emotional things like that aren't always logical. How can you be sure he wouldn't bend the truth a little to get some payback. Maybe he doesn't see how it will hurt."

"He wouldn't bend the truth, because I wouldn't let him get away with it. If you're right, and he has a little extra motivation, I can't see how that's bad."

Maybe Marris was crooked, but he was right about Seth. The man was playing it all ways, making sure no matter what happened with this case, he would smell pretty in the end.

Static fuzzed in her ear. "Hello?"

A crackle or two more, and Seth's voice was back. "Is that all you have?"

"I was wondering if you could have someone run a license number for me."

Nick's head snapped toward her. His brows rose in a silent question.

She nodded. She'd only been able to see the first three digits, but a partial and a description of the SUV was better than nothing. "Colorado plates."

"This has something to do with Raymond?"

"It would be helpful. That's all." Maybe she should have called someone else. The last thing she wanted to do was deal with a grilling from Seth. Especially since she might lose phone service at any time. But with the strain between the D.A.'s office and the police that this investigation business had caused, she wasn't sure she could get the quick results she needed unless she went through her own office.

As if to underscore the urgency, static hissed over the phone once again.

"You need to give me more than that."

"It was a red SUV, a Honda. 462 is all I caught."

Nick gave her a smile, and she returned it.

"That's not what I mean by more."

"It tried to run us down. Is that what you want to know?"

"Tried to run you…us…when did this happen?"

"Right after we talked to Marris."

"Marris? Damn."

Apparently it occurred to Seth that Marris might be behind that wheel, as well. "What are you going to do, Seth?"

The connection fuzzed again. When it came back, Seth's voice rang firm and commanding. "…to quit fooling around, Melissa. Get Raymond and his son in here immediately."

"I've tried, Seth. He doesn't want any part of protective custody, and I have to say, I can understand where he's coming from."

Nick nodded, glancing from the road to her and back.

"You can understand? When he and the kid are dead, will you understand then?"

Melissa's throat closed. She looked at Nick, glanced out of the corner of her eye at Jason in the backseat. This was enough. They couldn't risk their lives any longer. She couldn't risk them. Seth was right about that.

"Are you there?" Seth growled through another batch of static.

"Yes."

"Get him in here now. Him and the boy."

"I…" She met the glance from Nick. "…he doesn't

know who to trust, Seth. You've got to admit, things are pretty confusing."

"He might be confused. But you damn well shouldn't be. Get Raymond and the boy in here. If they aren't in protective custody by tomorrow, you no longer have a job."

Chapter Fifteen

It only took Melissa a minute to find the place where Jimmy had stashed his first-aid kit. She pulled out the collection of equipment and bandages and whatnot that probably rivaled that of some small-town clinics from one of the few kitchen cabinets and set to work on Nick's arm.

"What, did he plan to open a hospital?"

Melissa forced a chuckle, despite the tremor inside her chest that had only grown since talking to Seth. "Tammy is a nurse. She made sure he was well supplied."

From all she could tell, Nick's bone wasn't broken badly. The bone didn't seem to be protruding, anyway. She was a little coarse when it came to setting broken bones. But even Nick himself, who had a lot more experience tending to the wounds of animals, thought it wasn't bad. She strapped it into the soft cast and spilled a couple of painkillers onto her palm. "Take these."

"No thanks. I don't like the way they make me feel."

"You're going to like the pain of a broken arm even less."

"It's not so bad."

Right. He turned pale every time she'd moved it to adjust the cast. "It'll get worse. Your body is probably still pumping a good amount of adrenaline. When that wears off, you'll wish you'd taken these."

"Okay. Fine." He held out a hand and she gave him the pills, followed by a glass of water.

So far so good on her quest to take care of Nick and his son. She waited until after they ate another one of Tammy's casseroles and Nick tucked Jason safely into bed before she brought up the rest.

A fire crackling in the fireplace, she joined Nick on the lumpy couch. "I'm going to meet with Seth tomorrow." She wasn't going to mention what he'd said about her job, Seth's promise of a pink slip if she didn't have Nick and Jason in tow. Nick would only want to do something to fix it, even though there was nothing he could do.

"Okay."

"I'm going to walk down the road until I can get cell service, and I'm going to call a cab."

"You can take the truck."

"No. I can't."

He stared at her. A muscle along his jaw tensed under razor stubble.

"You need to go. Somewhere. Away from here."

He said nothing, just looked away from her, focusing on the fire.

Something stirred inside her, that warm, jittery feeling she always got when she looked at him. The soul-deep eyes. The little cleft in his chin. The brim of his hat cast shadows on his face that shifted and danced in the flicker of flame. She breathed deeply, trying to detect the scent of his skin.

All she could smell was smoke from the open hearth.

She resisted the urge to lean toward him, rest her head on his good shoulder, take in one last breath. There hadn't been anything between them. Nothing but a single kiss, a few words and a very short amount of time. Yet it was hard to let go. Hard to accept there would be nothing more. That whatever impossible fantasies she'd harbored had reached their end.

She had to let go of them. So did he. "I know you said you wanted to be there for me. But you have to be there for your son first. He's not safe here. You're not safe. What happened today is proof."

He looked back, his eyes meeting hers. "So come with us."

"I have a job to do."

"You're suspended."

She shook her head. That wasn't the half of it. When she didn't bring Nick and Jason into the D.A.'s office, she'd probably have no job at all. But even without a title or paycheck or any official authority, she still had work to finish. "I have to find out what's really going on. It's bigger than the job. It's even bigger than owing Jimmy."

"It's who you are."

She nodded. He understood. Somehow she knew he would, and the fact that she'd been right made her feel all the more empty. "As much as the ranch is who *you* are."

He stared into the fire, as if letting her comment

sink in. When he returned his gaze, his eyes held a sheen that wasn't there before. "When I first met you, I thought you were like Gayle." He held up his good hand, as if asking her to stave off whatever conclusions his confession would engender.

She shrugged a shoulder. She didn't know Gayle. Maybe there was something in that statement she should take offense with. But from where she sat, she couldn't see it. Nick had married her, hadn't he? She was the mother of a splendid little boy. She had to admit, she kind of liked the comparison. It was the closest she could get to having him, being part of an amazing family, something she'd never known. "I look a little like her. I noticed that."

He nodded. "The hair. The willpower. But I thought that meant you also had her ambition."

She wasn't sure what image of her he saw. "I am ambitious."

"Not in the same way. You do your job because you believe in the work's value. You want to make a difference."

He didn't elaborate on his ex-wife and her motivations, and Melissa didn't ask. She didn't want to know. She just wanted to hold his words in her heart, the way he saw Melissa Anderson. No one else. The way she wanted to be seen.

He leaned his head against the back of the couch as if he no longer had the energy to keep it upright.

"You okay?"

"No."

"We need to go to the hospital."

"My arm isn't the problem."

She didn't believe that. She saw the pain in his face, even after the pills should have worked their magic. "If it isn't your arm, what is it?"

"I know I shouldn't say this. Hell, I shouldn't even be feeling it." He raised his head and looked at her.

His eyes appeared glassy. The painkillers, no doubt. But his face held something tender, something honest, something she'd never seen in a man's face before.

A chill traveled over her skin, the sensation having nothing to do with being cold. She didn't want him to go on, to say another word. And yet, she had to hear. She had to know. She had to feel it, even though it was somewhere she couldn't afford to let herself go.

"I'm..." He inhaled deeply, as if he needed the extra oxygen to fuel his courage.

A tremor seized just below her rib cage. She couldn't hear this. As much as she wanted to, she just... "Wait." She brought her fingers to his lips.

He raised his good hand, engulfing her hand, placing it on the back of his neck.

She should withdraw. Look away. Retreat to the other side of the room. She tangled her fingers in the short curls at his nape.

"I'm falling in love with you, Melissa." He said the words on a rush, pushing them out on a single breath.

She'd known it was coming. On some level, she'd even wished for it. But although the words curled inside her, warm and precious, she couldn't keep them. She couldn't make them her own. She shook her head. "No. You can't."

He nodded and brought his face close. "It's impossible. I know."

It *was* impossible. She hardly knew him, yet she knew him so well. She couldn't do this, yet she couldn't take her hand away, either.

"I know," he said, as if answering her thoughts.

"You have to leave. You and Jason."

"I know." His breath caressed her lips. "We'll leave tomorrow."

"Tomorrow."

She wasn't sure if he lowered his lips or if she pulled him to her, but his kiss was all she needed, all she wanted. His warmth filled the cold empty quake inside her. His lips moved against hers and her mouth answered, automatically, naturally.

She wanted more, so much more. She wanted to be naked, skin touching skin, nothing between them. She wanted to feel him, soak in his heat, his scent, his love while she still could.

Her fingers found the buttons on his shirt. One by one, she worked them free. She moved her hands inside, caressed warm, smooth skin. She wanted to take off his shirt, to feel all of him, kiss all of him.

She hesitated. "Jason."

"He sleeps like the dead."

Nick was right. In the time she'd known Jason, he'd never awakened on his own in the night. Not once.

He moved to slip out of his sleeves.

"Your arm. I don't want to hurt you."

He glanced at the makeshift cast. "I forgot. I forgot everything…everything but you."

She kissed him again, careful of his arm. She couldn't stop. She slipped off his Stetson and ran her fingers through his hair. She kissed his lips and his neck and the cleft in his chin, the burn of stubble making her lips tingle.

Once she'd thought his cowboy mannerisms and hat and boots were what drew her. She'd been so stupid. It was the man he was. His sharp mind. His big heart. The way he gave her just what she needed. Even if she didn't know what that was.

He tried to slip the top button of her blouse free with one hand. "Clumsy."

"Here." She covered his hand with hers and unbuttoned. He splayed his fingers across her belly as she let the blouse slide from her shoulders and unfastened her bra.

He sucked in a breath. His hand circled to her back and guided her toward him. His lips closed over her nipple. Teasing and sucking, stirring heat within her she longed for, but hadn't known it. Hadn't known it until now.

He moved from one breast to another, soft, gentle. Stubble rasped her skin, heated her blood, burned her.

She closed her eyes. This couldn't be happening. Shouldn't be happening. But it was. And tomorrow... tomorrow he would be gone. She'd be alone.

She reached for his belt, his jeans. Unfastening both, she tugged them down his legs. She wanted to show him how she felt. She couldn't say it. She couldn't live it. But she could show him now. While they were still together. While they still had time. She could show him and hope he'd remember, that she'd remember in the lonely time ahead. She took him in her hand, feeling his length, caressing the smooth skin.

His fingers flew to her waist, unbuttoning, unzipping.

She couldn't wait. She pushed her own trousers and panties down her legs. Slowly, she moved kisses over the hard ridges of his stomach and up his chest. Claiming his mouth with hers, she straddled him and took him inside.

He filled her, slowly, gently. And as she opened to him, tears filled her eyes and the room became nothing but watery shadow.

Pleasure and heat built between them and finally crashed over her, sweeping away thought, taking him with her. He said her name on a hoarse whisper and held her tight against his chest.

They stayed that way until their heartbeats slowed. Clinging to one another as long as they could. Joined. Finally Nick's lips moved against her cheek, whispering in her ear. "We can figure this out. We'll take our time. After this is over."

"After this is over." She parroted his words and kissed his cheek. Sitting back, she looked into his eyes.

It was a nice dream, but she knew that's all it could be. And the way he looked at her, she could tell he knew it, too.

The problem was bigger than this case. It was bigger than him leaving town and her having to stay. Sitting with him here, touching him, tasting him, loving him—it was everything she wanted. More than she wanted. More than she'd believed existed.

But no matter how good it felt to be in Nick's arms, to show him how she felt, she couldn't bear the thought of reaching for him one day, and finding nothing there.

And that was the feeling that surrounded her like the chill air as she moved away from him and pulled on her clothes.

NICK KNEW THE CABIN would be empty the next morning when he awoke from his drug-induced heavy sleep. But the cold light of day made the realization even worse than he'd anticipated.

He'd worried telling Melissa he loved her would push her away. He probably wouldn't have done it if not for the painkillers. But as it was, he doubted anything he said or didn't say could have changed things.

And that had him feeling more hopeless than anything else.

He stared out the cabin's plate glass window. Even though the view was fogged by moisture between the panes, he could see the white swirl of snow on the wind.

He didn't know why he did this to himself. It was as if he deliberately chose women who couldn't love him. Maybe he was protecting himself, in that way. If they couldn't love him because of where he lived, what he did, who he was, then it couldn't be his fault when things didn't work out.

Pitiful.

He popped a couple more painkillers and chased them with a glass of water from the rusty tap. These would have to be his last. He had to drive in a few hours and needed a clear mind. But at least for now he could dull the throb in his arm, in his chest. He could put off the full brunt of the pain a little longer.

He padded into the living room area, feet cold on the

hard floor. He tried not to think of what had happened last night, what he and Melissa had shared. He knew it would be painful today, looking back on what he'd tasted and what he'd lost. If he'd never known what it could feel like to be that close to her, his pain would be more manageable today. But there wasn't a chance he could have turned her down.

The fire had gone out hours ago, nothing but blackened remnants of the largest logs left. He picked up the poker and stabbed one of the logs, shifting it back into place. He and Jason would have to pack and clear out, but first, he'd build another fire. He wasn't sure Melissa would be coming back. He couldn't see it. She'd probably return to her apartment rather than stay here. But he didn't like the idea of the cabin, which had been so warm with Melissa here to be cold and empty, even for the few hours they had left. Not when he could change it with a few logs, some crumpled newspaper and a match.

He wrestled a log from the stack with his one good arm. Carrying it the few feet to the hearth, he let it fall with a thunk and punched it into place with the poker. So far so good.

He added another log, then another. A few scraps of kindling tucked here and there. Then he reached for the paper.

Something nudged his side. He pulled himself from his thoughts. Jason. The little guy was sitting on the hearth next to him, snuggling into his side. He looked down into those big blue eyes and gave his son the most smile he could muster.

"Where's Melissa?"

"She's gone, Buddy."

"She's erranding?"

Nick let himself smile. Brilliant kid, his son. He needed to tell the little guy the truth. There was no point in letting him wait for her to return. "Not today. Melissa isn't coming back, Jason."

He scrunched up his brow. "Did she die? Like Mommy?"

"No, she didn't die. She just had to go back to the city."

"I like the city."

He knew it was just an observation on Jason's part, but it stabbed into him all the same. "I know you do."

"You're sad."

"Yes, I am."

"'Cause Melissa is gone?"

"Yes."

His lips turned down and his eyes grew red around the edges. "I miss her."

Nick ruffled a hand in Jason's wavy hair. "I miss her, too, Jason." Something caught in his throat, and for a moment, he couldn't speak.

Jason stared out the cabin's window at the snow falling and nodded. Then he looked back up into Nick's eyes. "I don't want you to be sad."

"Thanks, Buddy."

"I'll stay here with you."

Nick's eyes burned. Jason was a good kid, just making the offer because he didn't want Nick to be sad. Little did he know how much that offer meant. "Thanks. That is really nice. I know you like the city."

"I like the horses, too. Like at your ranch."

"I'm glad to hear it."

Jason shrugged his little shoulders. "I like to be where Melissa is. But I like to be where you are, too."

His words hit Nick like a hard kick to the head. What an idiot he'd been. He'd told Melissa he was the ranch, but that wasn't true. All along he'd expected her to change as he'd expected Gayle to change. It was him who was obsessed with a certain place, a certain life. If he really thought about it, wherever Jason was was exactly where he wanted to be. And if he really wanted to see if he and Melissa had a future together, after all this was over and Jason was safe, he needed to be where she was.

He slipped his arm around Jason and hugged his warm little body close. "You're brilliant, do you know that?"

"Brilliant?"

"Yes." He kissed the soft hair on the top of his head and pushed himself up from the hearth.

So much for moping around feeling sorry for himself. Being with the people he loved was more important to him than his location or his lifestyle or anything else. It was even more important than being able to explain away rejection. It was everything. And it was time he proved that to Melissa. It was time he proved it to himself.

If he was willing to take a chance, maybe she would be willing, too. At least he had to try. "I have to call Melissa."

"Are you going to tell her she has to stay here with us?"

"No. You and I are going to go on a little vacation. How does that sound?"

Jason's forehead scrunched low.

"And after that, I'm going to tell her we want to come back and stay with her. Does that sound better?"

Jason beamed as brightly as if it were Christmas morning. "It's great."

Nick located his suitcase and rummaged through it for his cell phone.

"Daddy?"

A thrill shot through Nick's chest at the sound of that word coming from Jason's lips. Just like it did every single time. It took a second for him to register the distress in the little voice.

He whipped around to see the boy staring at the newspaper Nick had been crumpling to help kindle the fire. "What is it, Buddy?"

Jason looked up. His little face crumpled. Tears streamed down his cheeks.

"What's wrong?" Nick crossed the room in two strides. He knelt down by Jason's side and gathered him close. His son's arms wrapped tightly around his neck.

Nick looked down at the paper Jason had been staring at, expecting to see an old story about Gayle's death. Nothing but a smattering of headlines about the upcoming elections met his gaze. "Jason? What has you so upset?"

Jason pushed back from his shoulder. "He yelled at Mommy. He made her cry."

Nick scanned the paper again. "Who did?"

"Mommy's boyfriend." He extended a plump little finger and pointed directly at a photo of Deputy District Attorney Seth Wallace.

Chapter Sixteen

Despite walking forever through a mountain of snow before she could get a phone signal to call for a cab, Melissa thought she reached the office early, before anyone else would be there.

She was wrong.

"I trust you brought Raymond and his son?" Seth leaned on the doorjamb of his office. His suit was perfectly pressed, his shirt white, his tie its usual assertive red. But the dark circles under his eyes testified he'd gotten about as much sleep as she had the past few days.

"Seth…"

"You didn't bring them in."

"I told you. Nick doesn't trust the system."

"And I told you that you wouldn't have a job."

"Then fire me."

He glanced away.

Strange. She'd never known Seth to make empty threats. If he played chicken, he won. In the courtroom and in life. Even if that meant he crashed and burned. "What's going on, Seth?"

He shook his head. "This whole thing. I thought I

could manage it. But wherever I turn, someone is screwing things up. Never counted on one of those screwups to be you."

"If you're after a neat and tidy witch trial for Jimmy and a witness who might end up dead under our protection, I suppose I am screwing things up." She knew she was taking a risk, talking to him like that. But she didn't want to hold back. Seth had to see what he was doing here. This everything-for-politics course he was choosing couldn't go on. "Is someone looking into Essie's background? Who she knew? All that?"

He didn't answer.

"Seth?" She pulled in a breath, trying to calm herself. The stress must be getting to Seth as it was to her. Both of them needed to mellow out and take this investigation step by step. "You remember what we talked about last night on the phone, don't you? You said you'd pass it along?"

"Yes, yes." He waved the back of his hand at her as if shooing a fly.

"So you called the P.D.? Or is someone in the office looking into it?"

"I sent it over to the gang unit."

Okay. So why hadn't he said that right away? "Are you okay, Seth?"

"Okay? Why wouldn't I be?"

"You seem…stressed."

He gave her a dry look. "And you're as relaxed as some kind of Zen master."

He had a point. The past few days had been hard on them both. "Did you call in that partial license plate?"

Again, no response.

What was going on with him? "You didn't call it in, did you?"

"It was a partial, Melissa. And you don't even have any witnesses to the vehicle going after you."

"Witnesses?" Was he serious? "How about Nick Raymond? How about me?"

"You and Raymond? Witnesses? As if the two of you are impartial observers?" He rolled his eyes. "Next you're going to be basing a whole case on that four-year-old kid, pretending he's some kind of witness."

Four-year-old kid? Witness? She shook her head. Whatever was going on with Seth, he wasn't making any sense.

Or was he?

"Seth, why are you bringing up Jason Raymond as a witness?"

He tilted his head back. "Oh, for God's sake. What kind of tangent are you off on now?"

"Not a tangent. It's what you said." His words shuffled into place in her mind. "You told me Jimmy was the target of the drive-by shooting. Why did you say that?"

"Because he was."

"Was he? Why? Why do you think that?"

"Calhoun explained it to you."

"I know what Calhoun explained. He explained his theory of what happened. But he had pitiful little evidence to back any of it up."

"He has evidence."

"What evidence? What evidence do you have that

Jimmy was the target? Why not Essie? Why not me? Why not Jason Raymond?"

He shuddered a little when she said Jason's name. Not a conscious reaction. Nothing like that. It was something purely physical.

"Did Jason see something, Seth?"

"The kid? No. I mean, what would he see?"

The murder? No. Jason showed some signs of trauma, especially when they'd first found him. But it was nothing that would suggest he'd seen something as horrible as his mother's murder. So what did Jason see?

"Her boyfriend. Jason saw Gayle's boyfriend."

Seth nodded. "Jimmy Bernard."

"No. Not Jimmy. It couldn't be. Jason was around Jimmy afterward. After the murder. That was the first time he'd met Jimmy. I was there." Why hadn't she thought of this sooner? How could she have just blindly swallowed the story Seth and Calhoun had force-fed her? "The landlord said the guy was tall, older, good-looking. Jimmy wasn't the only man who fit that description, Seth. You fit it, too."

"That's ridiculous."

"Jimmy wasn't Gayle's boyfriend. It was you. You were the one having an affair with Gayle."

Seth shook his head, disgust twisting his mouth and furrowing his brow. He circled behind his desk and sat down. "You really are set on screwing things up, aren't you? And I thought you were one I could count on."

Count on? She'd counted on Seth. She'd taken what he'd told her as fact. "You killed her. You killed Gayle Rodgers. Why, Seth? Was she going to tell your wife?

Was she going to tell the press? Was she going to ruin your bid for D.A.?"

Red suffused his face. "I worked too hard. I couldn't let her do it. I couldn't let her..."

"So you killed her? Because she was going to tell?"

"It was an accident. She was threatening to go public unless I got a divorce. I just got so angry. I didn't mean to."

No. That wasn't right.

The room whirled around Melissa. She gripped the back of the chair, desperate to maintain her balance. Gayle's murder and the framing of José Sanchez couldn't possibly be explained as an accident. His fingerprints were on the decorative statuette that had killed her. Somehow Seth must have planted them there, maybe even *before* the murder.

Melissa's chest constricted, making it hard to breathe. Gayle wasn't the only one Seth had killed. He'd recruited the four gangster wannabes. He'd staged the drive-by. "*You* hired those men to kill Essie and Jimmy, too. Seth? Didn't you? *You* tried to kill Nick and his son." She reached for her gun...and touched her empty hip.

He stood up from his desk, his fist in front of him. In his hand he held her gun. The barrel pointed straight at her chest.

Her cell phone rang in her bag, the muffled tweet barely audible over the pounding of her heart.

She had figured it out. Finally. But she'd done it far too late.

Chapter Seventeen

Melissa's phone rang four times before it switched Nick to voice mail. Where in the hell was she? He left a message for her to call him and hung up.

"Where's Melissa?"

He glanced into the rearview mirror. "I'm trying to find her, Buddy."

He squinted through the smeary windshield at the Denver skyline. She'd said she was going to the office. Precisely where Seth Wallace would presumably be headed this morning. Nick had hoped to head her off, to warn her before she met with her boss.

He prayed he wasn't too late.

He pulled up the Denver directory on his hand-held and punched in the number for the district attorney's office. The phone rang forever, it seemed. He was about to hang up and just race down to the building and bust in when a receptionist picked up. "Denver district attorney's office. How may I direct your call?"

"I need to speak to Melissa Anderson."

"Ms. Anderson is not in yet this morning. If you like, you can leave her a voice mail."

"I already have. Thanks." He paused for a moment.

The move was tricky. The last thing he wanted was for Wallace to know he was on to him. But if it was the only way he could reach Melissa, he had to take a shot. "Melissa said she would be meeting with Deputy District Attorney Seth Wallace this morning. Can you tell me if he's in?"

"He is. And he's been in a meeting since before I arrived. So that might be where Ms. Anderson is. I'll transfer you."

"Wait."

The phone clicked over.

Nick gripped his BlackBerry hard enough to make the casing creak. He'd expected her to ask who was calling before switching him over. The fact that she hadn't had him worried. He'd never thought about it before, but he'd wager the D.A.'s office had caller ID. She hadn't had to ask. One look at her phone readout, and she'd known who was on the other end of the line. No doubt soon Seth Wallace would, too.

Nick hadn't had time to catch his breath when Wallace's voice boomed over the line. "Raymond. Glad to hear from you. Where are you? I'll get some deputies out to you right away."

And not gangster wannabes? Nick bit back the response. "Is Melissa with you?"

"Yes. She is."

"Can I talk to her?"

"Not at the moment. What is this about? How can we help make this easier for you?"

Turn your murdering scumbag self in? Nick had to think. When he'd called, he'd been so focused on telling Melissa the truth about her boss, he hadn't planned any further ahead than that. "I have some papers here. Papers my ex-wife sent to me. Melissa said you needed them to help with the prosecution of her murderer."

"Yes. Yes, we do. Where are you? I'll send someone to pick them up."

"Not necessary. I'll bring them to you."

"Here? To the office?"

"Can you put Melissa on the line?"

"Tell you what. I believe Melissa mentioned to you that we have a few issues regarding security. I don't want to put you and your son in any kind of danger. So why don't you stay put, and Melissa can come and pick up the papers? She can also bring some extra security to make sure you and your son stay protected."

Him and his son. All along Melissa and he had both assumed Nick was the one who was in danger. That Jason was too young to be a witness, too young to be a threat. And all along, Jason was the one who could identify Wallace as Gayle's boyfriend.

Anger rifled through Nick. Right this minute, he felt as if he could storm into that office and take Wallace out with one bare hand.

He forced his breathing to slow. He couldn't let emotion get the best of him. Not now. "I'd like to talk to Melissa."

"Sorry. She just ran out of the office. It's crazy around here this morning. But I'll give her the message immediately. Where are you?"

Something had happened to Melissa. Wallace had done something. Nick knew it. She would be picking up her phone otherwise. He couldn't quite believe Wallace would hurt her. Not right there in the office. But if he could get her somewhere else? Nick wouldn't put it past him.

Think.

"Raymond?"

He could meet with Wallace. Choose a safe place. Maybe even find a way to call in Detective Marris or someone else to help. Find a way to make them believe the chief deputy D.A. was a murderer. A cop killer.

A weight settled into his stomach. It would be a hard sell. Maybe impossible without any evidence except a story about his four-year-old recognizing a photo in the newspaper. Lord knows, he'd have trouble buying it.

His son. He glanced into the rearview.

Jason stared out the window, thumb in mouth and fingers twirled in hair.

He had to find a safe place for Jason. That was the first thing. No matter what happened next, Wallace was not going to get his hands on Nick's son. "Okay. Tell Melissa I'll meet her."

"Good, where?"

He scanned through his limited knowledge of Denver. He'd seen very little of the city besides the hotel where the shooting took place and the McDonald's playland. But years ago he'd been here with Gayle. He remembered a bookstore. The Tattered Cover, if he recalled correctly.

No. He didn't just need a crowd of people. He needed more. Some kind of law presence. A bookstore wouldn't cut it. "The train station downtown."

"Union Station?"

"Yes."

"Okay. I'll have Melissa meet you at the Wynkoop Street entrance. She can be there in twenty minutes."

Too soon. He had too much to do before then. "I will be there in ninety."

MELISSA DIDN'T KNOW if Seth hadn't thought about the construction going on at the train station, or if it was part of his plan. But either way, the area around Union Station was a mess. Seth wove his Mercedes slowly through construction barriers and snarls of traffic. She sat in the passenger seat, her cuffed hands in her lap, and stared out the window, searching for any sign of Nick.

Her mind was still whirling with what she'd figured out about Seth. That he'd killed Gayle with his own hands, paid those men to kill Jason, only Jimmy and Essie had gotten caught in the cross fire. "Tell me, Seth. Was Jimmy one of the people who screwed things up for you? Was he getting close? Is that why you had to unleash Calhoun in an attempt to discredit him?"

"You want me to tell you all the details, Melissa? Really?"

"Why not? I doubt you're planning to let me go. Was it you driving that red SUV last night, too? Where did you get it? Would the license number lead back to you?"

He gave her a dismissive look and cranked the volume on the car's stereo. The strong yet brutal strains of Wagner washed her questions away.

Fine. She didn't need the answers. Not from him. She'd figured out most of it anyway. After she'd gotten hold of that first piece, one thing had just led to another.

Why she hadn't seen it all before—before Jimmy and Essie had died, before she'd ended up at gunpoint, before Seth had set up Nick to walk into a trap—would haunt her the rest of her life.

A span of time that promised to be pretty short.

She spotted Nick before Seth did. There he was, in front of the historic Union Station, bent as if examining the day's headlines in the newspaper vending machines out front. The box of Gayle's papers sat at his feet.

Seth made a strangled sound in his throat. "Damn it. Damn it. Where the hell is the kid?"

She let out a breath she hadn't been aware she was holding. So Nick was aware that something was wrong. She'd prayed he wouldn't totally trust Seth. In the past couple of hours she'd reviewed every statement she'd ever made to Nick regarding the chief deputy, hoping she hadn't conveyed her blind trust to him, hoping he'd see past her misplaced confidence.

Seth piloted the car to the curb. He hit a button on his armrest. Her window lowered.

The chocolate cakelike scent of malt from the nearby Wynkoop Brewing Company wafted into the car. The sweet smell she'd always found comforting now stuck in the back of her throat.

Nick lifted the box with his good arm and approached the car. He stopped ten feet from the door. "Can you help me with this, Melissa?"

"Get in the car." Seth's order rang out like a bark.

Nick didn't move. He focused on Melissa.

She gave him what she hoped was a warning look.

His expression didn't change. "This damn box is heavy. I can't get it into the car with one arm."

Seth raised the gun just enough for Nick to get a glimpse. "Melissa needs you to get into the car. You and the box. If you want to help her, you're going to have to find a way to manage it."

Nick's mouth flattened to a hard line.

Seth hit a button on the dash. A click sounded in the back of the car. "Put the box in the trunk. And don't try anything. Melissa needs you to be very careful in what you do. Remember that."

Nick circled to the back of the trunk and dropped the box inside. He used his good hand to slam it closed with a thunk.

Seth peered into the mirrors, tracking Nick's progress. His hand was tight on the gun, his knuckles white with strain. He was inexperienced with firearms. He didn't have the training she did. If she could distract him, take his attention off the weapon in his hand, she might be able to disarm him. The trick was, doing it with her hands cuffed. And not getting shot in the process.

"Get in. Make it fast," Seth ordered.

Nick opened the door behind her and slipped into the backseat.

"Give me the handgun," Seth said.

"What handgun?"

"The one stuffed in your waistband."

Melissa's mind raced. So Nick had brought a gun? What gun? The only gun they had was the rifle he'd carried with him from the ranch. That and her handgun. The one that was now pointing at her chest.

"I want the gun. And if you want to help Melissa or

even just have her continue breathing, you need to give it to me."

A handgun clattered against the plastic console between the front seats. A handgun that looked awfully familiar.

Seth grabbed it with his non-gun hand and tucked it away.

Melissa glanced around the car. Surely someone had to see them. They had to question what was going on. But the construction barriers fenced most pedestrians off a distance away from them. And even if they did think they caught a glimpse of a gun out of the corner of their eyes, who would believe an ugly scene like this was going on inside a Mercedes like Seth's?

Seth tossed a set of handcuffs into the back. "Put these on. And Melissa needs you to get them tight." Seth watched the mirror.

Melissa heard the cuffs rattle in the seat behind her.

"What's going on here?" Nick asked, his voice a low growl. "I thought you were going to provide protection."

"I thought you were going to bring your son."

"It was Jason you wanted all along, wasn't it?"

"Melissa needs you to shut up."

Melissa's throat felt thick. So Nick had figured it out. He'd known Seth was behind it all, and yet he'd come to this sham of a meeting anyway. Some investigator she'd turned out to be. Some protector. She hadn't figured a damn thing out, even though the murderer was right in her own office. And when she had, not only had it been too late, she'd dragged Nick into this mess with her.

Seth shifted the car into gear. He drove through city streets, calm as if on a Sunday drive. But if she looked close, she could see his lower lip and chin tremble. Both the knuckles of his left hand on the wheel and his right on the gun showed white. His voice had a desperate edge, as if he was trying hard to portray a command he felt was slipping away.

Melissa scanned the landscape outside. Seth was on the edge. The disheveled look. The desperation bubbling under the surface. The complete failure of coping with her questions back at the office. He was like a cornered animal, his whole carefully constructed scheme coming down around his ears. And that made him more dangerous and unpredictable than ever. People walking on the streets outside, people driving their cars, children in the backseat, all of them could become victims if she wasn't careful. All of them could pay the price for her mistake of trusting the wrong person.

She held her breath, willing Nick to keep quiet, to not say anything to agitate Seth until they were clear of so many potential victims.

"Those guys I saw. You paid them to kill Jason. And when they shot Jimmy instead, you decided to pin the whole mess on him."

Seth said nothing, but his fingers tightened further. The lines bracketing his mouth dug deep as ravines.

"You often kill your mistresses? Keep them from talking?"

They hummed onto the highway. Cars swirled around them. A compact pulled alongside, a mother with two toddlers strapped in the backseat. A wheel jerked to the side or a bullet fired through the door, and their busy morning would instantly become a tragic one.

"You often pay losers to kill a four-year-old? Or just if you have to keep him from telling anyone that you hurt his mommy?"

Seth took an exit that led to the area where they'd met Marris yesterday. He drove past the tavern and wound up the mountainside.

"You're man enough to kill a woman and try to kill her kid, and yet you can't even own up to what you've done?"

Melissa shifted in her seat. All drive long, Nick had been provoking Seth, needling him as if trying to get a reaction. He wouldn't do that for no reason. He wouldn't meet Seth and get into the car in the first place if he didn't have a plan. Not Nick. He didn't lash out blindly. He wasn't like that at all. He was a man one could rely on.

A man she could trust.

Shivers flooded her skin. She was so stupid. She was so blind. When she should have been skeptical, she'd taken Seth at his word. And when she should have trusted, she'd pushed Nick away.

She glanced in the back.

A blue-jeaned thigh shifted into view. He scooted his body toward the center, only an inch, but it was enough to show her what he intended to do.

It was risky, she knew. She could end up dead. In this terrain, they all could. But she sure as hell didn't have a plan. And if she didn't trust Nick's, the two of them would wind up dead for sure.

"Jimmy figured it out. Or at least he was going to."

Melissa took a deep breath and pressed on. "With all your experience in the system, all the criminals you've prosecuted, I'd think you'd be better at pulling something like this off."

"I fooled your precious Jimmy for a long time, and I sure as hell fooled you."

"And now you're going to kill Nick and me?"

In the backseat, Nick shifted a little more.

She wasn't sure how he was going to do anything with one arm broken and his hands cuffed. She swallowed into a dry throat. "I don't know what good you think this is all going to do, Seth. Too many people are figuring things out. It's not just us."

He glanced her way. Beads of sweat hung at his hairline. "Like who?"

"Ben Marris."

"I wasn't kidding when I said we have evidence that Marris is being paid off. You were right about Jimmy Bernard. But Marris? Dirty as a damn whore." He took a hairpin turn. A canyon opened up to the right of the car.

Was he bluffing? She didn't think so. With any luck, it wouldn't matter. "How about Calhoun? He's an ass, but he can be a good investigator. He's going to add things up."

"Calhoun will spend the rest of his career trying to prove Jimmy Bernard was on the take. You think I was driving that witch hunt, as you put it?" He shook his head. He steered the car around another tight curve.

Melissa could see the guardrail whizzing by on the left, nothing but air behind it.

"An investigation into Jimmy Bernard is Calhoun's

wet dream. He's never going to even glance at anything that ruins it for him."

He was probably right. "Tammy won't rest. Not until Jimmy's cleared."

"Tammy Bernard?" A smile spread over Seth's lips.

A smile that made Melissa's blood chill to ice. What had she said? What had she done?

"Tammy Bernard. How very convenient. Finally I can tie up the last of the loose ends. Tammy Bernard. Why the hell didn't I see it before? I'll bet she makes a wonderful babysitter." Seth glanced up into the rear view mirror. His smug expression flashed to startled.

He'd seen Nick, noticed he'd moved behind Seth in the backseat.

Using her two hands together like a club, Melissa struck at the gun.

A shot exploded, the sound cracking through Melissa's ears, her head, her whole body. The gun skittered to the floor, hitting hot on her ankle.

Seth's head slammed back against his head rest.

"The wheel!" Nick yelled. "Grab the wheel."

Not even thinking, Melissa lunged for the steering wheel. Hands bound, she struggled to right the car, a tight bend in the road coming up fast.

A gurgle ripped from Seth's throat. He thrashed his arms, beating at the back of Melissa's head and shoulders. He jammed his feet down on the floorboards.

The car accelerated.

A scream caught in Melissa's throat. She couldn't think. She couldn't breathe. She couldn't even pray.

The guardrail rushed at her.

She yanked the wheel to the side.

Tires shrieked. The car swayed. Something hit the back fender.

She countersteered. The car fishtailed and straightened. They'd made it. They were alive.

Another curve rushed up fast.

A blow from his fist clanged into her head, her shoulders. Another. Another. Faster. Harder.

The car bulleted for the next hairpin turn.

She had to get Seth's foot off the gas, but how? With her hands bound, it was all she could do to steer.

They screeched around the second turn, the back end whipping almost into a spin. Something crashed behind them. The guardrail.

Oh, God.

Seth's blows grew weaker. The car started to slow.

As Melissa piloted them around one more turn, the acceleration and Seth's fists stopped. Using both hands, she shifted the car manually into second gear, into first. Finally she guided the car into an overlook and jammed it into Park. They jolted to a stop.

She sat up, panting, and looked at Seth's purple face.

Nick released the ends of Seth's red tie and slumped forward against the back of her seat.

Chapter Eighteen

As much as Nick had wanted to kill Seth Wallace when he threatened Jason's life, he was relieved the man wasn't dead. After Melissa stopped the car and Nick released the necktie, they'd located the handcuff keys in his pocket. They released themselves and cuffed him, getting both wrists and ankles for good measure.

It was right, seeing Seth Wallace trussed up like a rodeo calf. It was right he was still alive and on his way to prison. Death would be too easy for a slime like him. No, he deserved the humiliation of going through the system he'd tried to manipulate. He deserved the headlines exposing the sleazy underbelly of his life. He deserved to be locked away with all the scumbags he'd put there before him.

He deserved justice.

And lucky for them, he had a GPS service in his fancy car.

They didn't have to wait long before the narrow overlook was flashing with lights from sheriffs' cars and an ambulance. Just a short time later, detectives rolled in. People he didn't know, but Melissa did. People who did the job because it was important, because it helped people.

People like her.

Nick pulled the tape recorder from his pocket and handed it to the first detective on the scene. "It's all there. Seth Wallace telling us what he did in his own words."

Melissa's eyebrows arched. A hint of a smile touched her lips for the first time since they'd said goodbye last night. "You recorded it? All of it?"

"Tammy's idea. If it was up to me, I would have just borrowed her gun and rushed in like a bull."

"Her gun. I knew I recognized that gun."

The detective left them with strict instructions to stay and wait for more questions. Nick nodded dutifully. Lovely.

He lifted his hat, forgetting he had no functioning second hand to rake through his hair. With nothing left to do, he plopped it back on his head and looked down at Melissa.

He had so much to say to her. So much he wanted her to know. But now, standing here, her beautiful eyes peering up at him, he had no clue where to start. He didn't remember any words. Not a single one.

She was the one who spoke first. "I'm so stupid. You saved me. I'm so stupid, and you saved me." Tears filled her eyes, spilled over and trickled in little rivers down her cheeks.

He had to smile, his own eyes getting a little watery. "You're as tongue-tied as me? This is one for the books."

"You're laughing at me?"

"Laughing with you, sweetheart." He reached out for her with his good arm and gathered her close. "Laughing with you. That's all I want."

He wanted to say more, to explain his change of heart, to make his case. But he could sense this wasn't the time for making decisions about the rest of their lives. It was the time for holding each other. For being grateful they were alive. For counting all the blessings of this world.

She craned her neck and looked up at him, and he brought his lips down to hers. Salt and warmth and Melissa. If he could kiss these lips forever, he'd be happy to the end of his days.

He just had to find a way to convince her of that.

AFTER ALL THE questioning and the follow-up and all the other details Melissa had had to tend to, two days passed before she was able to spend some time with Jason and Nick. Tammy had insisted on putting them up at her house, and Nick had given in. The arrangement had been good for all three of them. Melissa could see it in their faces when she'd come to dinner the second night. Nick and Jason had someone to dote on them after all they'd been through, and Tammy had someone to serve. All three looked happy. At peace for the first time since this mess had begun.

Melissa only wished she was in such good shape.

She'd spent most of the night playing with Jason, and all of them had gotten so wrapped up in the fun that they'd almost forgotten to eat. Jason settled for a peanut butter and jelly sandwich and was now getting pajama-ed with Nick and reading with Tammy, whom he now called Mee-Maw. Their nightly routine, two nights old. Melissa had set to grilling three steaks for the adults' dinner.

"You'd make a great cowboy."

His voice startled her. She hadn't heard the door slide open. "A cowboy? How so?"

He walked across the deck, his boots ringing hollow on the wood. "Lots of grilling under the stars in the guest-ranch business." He smiled. "Kidding. I know you love your job, that you love it here in the city."

She glanced around. The buildings of downtown glowed in the distance, the shadows of mountains looming beyond. But up above them, the sky stretched like a blank slate, waiting for the stars to write something new.

"So Jason and I have talked about another possibility." He stopped next to her and pulled his hat off by the crown with his good hand, his good arm, the other now properly set in a cast. He fidgeted with the brim, then adjusted it back on his head. "I want you to take a second to just hear it out, if you would."

She watched him closely, a hum settling over her nerves. "Sure. What is it?"

"We're talking about moving. Here."

"To Denver?" She squinted up at him. She couldn't have heard him right.

"Is that a problem?"

"Yes."

"Yes? Why?"

"You're a rancher. You love the Circle J. You'd be miserable living in the city."

"I'd be more miserable without you."

She blinked her eyes, chasing back the surge of tears. There could be nothing in the world more romantic than a man willing to give up everything he owned, everything he was, so he could be with you. But as lovely as the feeling was, it wasn't what she wanted. She'd fallen in love with him. Nick Raymond, the man. And if she took the ranch out of Nick, eventually there'd be nothing left of that man he was.

Besides, she had other plans. "You can't give up the Circle J."

"Why not? If I've figured out anything throughout this whole mess, it's that people are a lot more important to me than places. And I'm never going to get that mixed up again."

He brought his lips down to hers, tasting, caressing. A short little kiss that left her hungry for more.

She smiled up at him, wondering if her eyes were twinkling like the first stars in the wide open sky. "There's another reason you can't give up the ranch and move to the city."

"What's that?"

"Because I have a job interview with a sheriff's department up in Wyoming. Teton County."

"What?"

"I want to go back to what is important to me. Helping people. Protecting people. The hands on part of justice. Not running down details for the D.A."

He let out a chuckle. "So that's what your job is about? Running down details?"

"Not is, *was*. I quit."

His eyes rounded. "You quit your job?"

"I couldn't go back there. Not after all that's

happened. There's no part of me that even wants to. I need a change of scenery."

The smile started with his eyes then spread to his whole face. "I know a place that has great scenery. Or at least it will once you're there."

Oh, God. If he threw a tilt of the hat or a "Howdy, ma'am" in there, she was toast. As it was, she felt as if she might just swoon.

His smile dimmed. "You okay?" He cupped her elbow with his hand.

"Yeah. I'm more than okay, as long as I can catch my breath. This is all happening a little fast."

He nodded. "I have guest cabins. I've never rented one out on more than a weekly basis, but I'm sure it can be arranged. I'm pretty close with the boss."

"You would do that?"

"Let you get your feet wet, decide if it's what you really want? Absolutely. And the rest…the rest we'll just take day by day, okay?"

She shot him a teasing smile. "One day is all you can handle?"

His eyes darkened a shade, deepened. "No. That's not all I can handle. It's not all I want. I want more. I know that even now. I want the rings and the wedding vows, and I want the promises of forever. But before any of that, I want you to be sure that you want that, too. And I'm willing to wait as long as it takes—'til I'm as old as those mountains, if need be—for you to be sure. For *us* to be sure."

"You'd do that?"

"Only for you, darling. Only for you."

He kissed her again, this time slow and deep. And

for the first time in her life she knew she had found what she wanted. What she needed. What she never even really knew existed before. She'd found a home. She'd found a family. And she'd found someone she could trust to be there whenever she needed to reach out her hand.

* * * * *

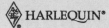 HARLEQUIN®

INTRIGUE

COMING NEXT MONTH

Available August 10, 2010

LARGER-PRINT BOOKS!

GET 2 FREE LARGER-PRINT NOVELS

◆ HARLEQUIN®

INTRIGUE®

PLUS 2 FREE GIFTS!

Breathtaking Romantic Suspense

HARLEQUIN®

A Romance

FOR EVERY MOOD™

Spotlight on

Heart & Home

Heartwarming romances
where love can happen
right when you least expect it.

See the next page to enjoy a sneak peek
from Harlequin® American Romance®,
a Heart and Home series.

Five hunky Texas single fathers—five stories from Cathy Gillen Thacker's LONE STAR DADS *miniseries. Here's an excerpt from the latest,* THE MOMMY PROPOSAL *from Harlequin American Romance.*

"I hear you work miracles," Nate Hutchinson drawled. Brooke Mitchell had just stepped into his lavishly appointed office in downtown Fort Worth, Texas.

"Sometimes, I do." Brooke smiled and took the sexy financier's hand in hers, shook it briefly.

"Good." Nate looked her straight in the eye. "Because I'm in need of a home makeover—fast. The son of an old friend is coming to live with me."

She was still tingling from the feel of his warm palm. "Temporarily or permanently?"

"If all goes according to plan, I'll adopt Landry by summer's end."

Brooke had heard the founder of Nate Hutchinson Financial Services was eligible, wealthy and generous to a fault. She hadn't known he was in the market for a family, but she supposed she shouldn't be surprised. But Brooke had figured a man as successful and handsome as Nate would want one the old-fashioned way. *Not that this was any of her business…*

"So what's the child like?" she asked crisply, trying not to think how the marine-blue of Nate's dress shirt deepened the hue of his eyes.

"I don't know." Nate took a seat behind his massive antique mahogany desk. He relaxed against the smooth leather of the chair. "I've never met him."

"Yet you've invited this kid to live with you permanently?"

"It's complicated. But I'm sure it's going to be fine."

Obviously Nate Hutchinson knew as little about teenage

boys as he did about decorating. But that wasn't her problem. Finding a way to do the assignment without getting the least bit emotionally involved was.

Find out how a young boy brings Nate and Brooke together in THE MOMMY PROPOSAL,
coming August 2010 from Harlequin American Romance.